THE UNEXPECTED GIFT

When love transcends borders and distance

Heidi Donohue

Editor: Emily Stark

- PROLOGUE -

I t's raining outside, the steady rhythm of droplets tapping against the window, mirroring the storm of emotions within me. While everyone else has headed downstairs for karaoke, I've chosen to stay back and study. I'm not quite sure what made me think I could focus; my mind has been wandering for weeks, and my declining grades are a testament to that struggle. The thought of socializing feels even more daunting right now.

So, I sit at my desk, staring at the picture of our last night together, one hand propped against my forehead and the other resting next to my silent phone, willing it to ring with Javier's number. Nearly three months have passed since our last conversation, but the memory of that painful call is still raw. The ache of his absence gnaws at me, making it impossible to concentrate on anything else.

I had been so hopeful, so sure that Javier's second visa application would be approved. But when I called, his voice thick with emotion, I knew something was terribly wrong. The consular officer had denied his request once again.

"I can reapply in a year," he told me, regret evident in his tone.

A year? My heart sank. I couldn't possibly wait that long. The past six months had been agonizing enough.

I miss everything about him—the way his cologne lingers in the air after he leaves a room, his infectious laugh, the warmth and safety of his strong embrace. Most of all, I miss the way he makes me feel—like the most beautiful girl in the world.

Our whirlwind romance had been the most genuine and passionate connection I had ever experienced. We promised to make our long-distance relationship work, but I never anticipated how challenging it would be to reunite back in my homeland. Deep down, I know I should never have left; staying would have made everything so much easier.

My professor warned me, but I chose to ignore the signs. Identifying me, his novia, as Javier's sponsor could imply he might try to overstay if temporary status was granted. What ties did he have to ensure he would return to his home country if the woman he loved was American and lived in the United States?

I feel like a fool for not listening, for letting my heart overrule my head. I had been so caught up in my desperation to see him that I had forgotten about the very real challenges we faced.

I've spent countless nights lying awake, replaying our conversation, wishing I could turn back time and change the outcome.

"Then I'll find another way," Javier vowed, determination lacing his words.

Another way? But how?

As if the delayed reunion were not enough, he now isn't returning my phone calls. *If he truly loves me, then why isn't he returning my calls?*

My mind races with doubts and fears. Maybe he's lost interest. Maybe the distance and struggle to reunite are too much. Maybe he's met someone else. Maybe there's always been someone else.

The rain continues to fall, each drop a reminder of the uncertainty and longing that fills my heart.

Pushing those insecurities aside, I square my shoulders, steel my nerves, and carefully dial the memorized international phone number: 0-1-1-5-9-3-4...

The line begins to ring, a series of harsh tones cutting through the silence of my room. With each passing ring, my heart races faster.

Beep...Beep...Beep...

This time, I promise myself. This time, if he answers, we'll find our way back to each other, no matter what obstacles stand in our way.

Beep...Beep...Beep...

As the ringing continues, I close my eyes and whisper, "Please, Javier...I need to hear your voice. I need you."

Beep...Beep...Bee—

The harsh tones are abruptly cut off as the line connects with a sharp click.

"¿Aló?"

Startled by the muffled sound of a woman's voice, I quickly hang up the phone, my heart pounding. I must have dialed the wrong number.

Taking a deep breath, I try the number again, but the same unfamiliar voice greets me once more.

I swallow hard and ask in Spanish, "Is Javier there?"

February 15, 1993
OPENING DOORS TO THE WORLD

With trembling hands, I slide a colorful brochure across the dining room table toward my parents, my heart pounding with a whirlwind of excitement and anxiety. "Señor Lopez asked me to stay after class today to give me this," I say, my voice quivering with anticipation. "He thinks I should apply."

"Study for a semester in South America," my mother reads aloud, her eyebrows raised in surprise.

"Why would you want to go to South America?" my father questions, his skeptical tone sending a wave of unease crashing over me.

I take a deep breath, preparing to explain. "My professor says it's the only way to truly immerse myself and learn another language," I say, my voice filled with a blend of hope and determination.

Even though they gave me their blessing to apply, I can sense a lingering doubt in their voices. Deep down, I don't think they truly believed I would follow through with it.

Reflecting on the application process, I am filled with pride as I recall the glowing letters of recommendation I've received. My teachers describe me as hard-working, organized, and well-spoken. Señor Lopez commends me for being motivated, curious, and open to new ideas. Another professor highlights my maturity, eagerness, and ambition to learn as much as I can about any topic presented.

In the last section of the application, I'm asked to explain why I want to study abroad. "Share your unique story," it prompts. I pour my heart into the essay, recounting the harrowing experience of undergoing surgery at fifteen to remove a benign tumor from my liver.

I describe the patience and determination required to push through the physical and emotional pain, the setbacks that strained my senior year of high school, and my decision to begin my studies at a local community college to stay close to home. I explain how these obstacles shaped my character, instilled a sense of purpose, and inspired me to make a meaningful impact on others.

I go on to share my aspiration to become a teacher. Beyond academic and professional growth, I express my belief that studying abroad will help me become a proficient Spanish speaker and a more culturally sensitive individual.

As I finish writing, I realize how much I truly want this opportunity. I'm not just saying I'm the perfect candidate for the program; I wholeheartedly believe it with every fiber of my being.

March 15, 1993
FROM APPLICATION TO ACCEPTANCE

I tremble with excitement as I gently peel open the envelope, my heart racing with anticipation. Clearing my throat, I begin reading aloud, "Dear Olivia Weber, we are delighted to inform you that you have been chosen for our Study Abroad program ..."

"Yes! I got accepted!" I exclaim, my voice bursting with joy. My eyes dart across the page, and I discover that I will be spending the semester in Ecuador.

Handing the letter to my parents, I watch their expressions shift as they scrutinize the contents, a blend of pride and concern flickering in their eyes.

"Are you really sure you want to do this?" my mother asks, her voice laced with worry as she reminds me that I won't know anyone there and that I have a fear of the dark.

Taking a deep breath, I gather my thoughts, feeling the weight of their concerns. "Yes, I'll be far from home, and yes, there will be challenges. But I'm not the same person I was before my surgery. I'm stronger now, more resilient, and eager to prove to myself and others just how much I can achieve."

"Three years ago, I learned to be grateful for every day," I continue, my voice filled with emotion. "You never know if there will be a tomorrow. This could be life-changing for me." I remind them about my surgery, the milestones I missed, and the perspective it gave me.

My father takes a deep breath, his expression softening. "Well, then I guess you are going to Ecuador," he says, a mixture of resignation and support in his tone.

Despite their worries, I feel a deep conviction in my heart that this is the right decision for me. I'm ready to embrace this new adventure, to immerse myself in a different culture, and to grow both personally and academically.

"Thank you," I say to my parents, throwing my arms around them and feeling the warmth of their love and support as I give them a heartfelt hug.

I snatch the phone from the receiver on the kitchen wall, my heart racing as I dial my best friend's number. I can barely contain my excitement, my fingers tapping nervously on the kitchen table as I wait for her to pick up.

With each ring, my anticipation builds. I steal a glance at my parents, who are still nearby, and give them a reassuring smile, silently thanking them again for their unwavering support.

Finally, I hear a click on the other end of the line, and Melanie's familiar voice fills the air. Without giving her a moment to say more than "Hello," I burst forth with my news, my words spilling out in a rush of enthusiasm.

"Melanie, you'll never guess what just happened! I got accepted into the Study Abroad program, and I'm going to Ecuador for a whole semester!"

I can't wait to share all the details with her and start planning for this incredible adventure.

April 11, 1993
GEARING UP FOR GLOBAL LEARNING

S itting on my bedroom floor, with Melanie sprawled out across my bed, I look closer at the application my host family submitted for review. "So, it says here my host family lives in Guayaquil," I say, excitement and anxiety bubbling inside me.

Melanie rolls onto her stomach, thumbing through a travel guide about Ecuador. She finds the section titled "Guayaquil." "Whoa, it says Guayaquil is the biggest city in the country, with, like, two million people."

"I'm gonna be living in a city?" I ask, surprised.

"Sounds like a pretty big deal. Way bigger than Harrisburg," Melanie points out.

"Yeah, in a foreign country where everyone speaks Spanish," I add, feeling a bit nervous.

"Come on, you know some Spanish," Melanie encourages.

"Not fluently," I remind her. Growing up in the middle of nowhere, I start to worry about how I'll get around. I've never taken public transportation and have no clue how to hail a cab.

Melanie asks what the application says about the family I'll be living with.

"Looks like there's a mom, dad, and two kids— Cristina, who's eight, and Enrique, who's three. And there's someone named Mayra, who I guess is the housekeeper. They have a dog, too."

Flipping through my Spanish-English dictionary, I figure out that Victor is an engineer, like my dad. Next to Ramona's name is the word 'comercio,' which means 'trade.' She also says she drives kids to school. "I'm guessing she's a bus driver," I say.

"Why not just call her a conductora de autobús?" Melanie asks.

Shrugging, I admit, "I don't know."

"Anything else?" she probes.

Reading in Spanish, I summarize what it says about their home. "They actually list electricity, water, and telephone. I wonder if that means not everyone has those."

"Ecuador is a third-world country. So, yeah, not every house has electricity or water. You might really be roughing it," Melanie points out.

"That's what I'm worried about," I reply, crossing my legs.

Melanie sits up, slides off the bed, walks up to me, and playfully shoves me like an inflatable punching bag.

"Ouch," I bounce back up, rubbing my arm. "That's where I got my shots!"

"Shots? What shots?" she asks, her curiosity piqued.

"I had to get a bunch of vaccines before leaving the country." Referring to the list of required immunizations, I rattle off, "Yellow fever, influenza, hepatitis A, typhoid, and rabies. Luckily, I was already up-to-date on hepatitis B, tetanus, and measles."

Melanie raises her eyebrows. "That's a lot."

"No kidding," I admit, my voice a mix of concern and resignation.

"Why would you pick a place that's so dirty and poor?" Melanie asks, bluntly.

"I didn't pick it! They chose the destinations for us," I explain, feeling a twinge of frustration.

"I admire you for wanting to explore new places. I just don't know if this trip is gonna be as great as you think it will be," she says, skepticism hanging in the air.

Similar questions swirl in my mind... *Am I making a mistake? Can I change my mind?*

"So, who else is going on this trip?" Melanie asks.

"I have no idea."

"You don't know anyone else going?"

"Nope."

"You really are crazy."

Maybe I am, I think to myself. But despite the doubts creeping in, there's still a bigger part of me that's excited for this adventure. I'm stepping into the unknown, and while it's scary, it's also thrilling. I take a deep breath, trying to push away the nerves. This is my chance to grow, to learn, to experience something completely new. Even if it's challenging, I know it'll be worth it.

In the weeks that follow, I dive into research, preparation, and packing for my big trip—getting traveler's checks, acquiring a passport, and buying multi-pack rolls of film for my 35mm Kodak camera. I stock up on sunscreen and bug spray, invest in an electrical travel adapter for my travel iron and hair dryer, and buy a cordless compact butane curling iron, just in case the electricity isn't always reliable.

May 14, 1993
Moments Before Departure

"Hey, would you mind taking our picture?" I ask a stranger in the airport waiting room.

"Sure thing, love," says the tall, slender blonde with a British accent.

Huddled together, she tells us, "Okay, say cheese!"

My parents and I shout 'cheese,' while Beth, my younger sister, giggles and adds, "Queso de queso," in a deep, husky voice, totally imitating the chihuahua from the Taco Bell commercials.

"Beth," my mother scolds, trying not to smile.

As my dad takes the camera back and thanks the stranger, I turn to Beth and ask, "Why do you always have to be such a smart aleck?"

Wrapping her arms around me, Beth teases, "Aw, come on, sis, you know you're gonna miss me." I playfully push her away, and as much as I don't want to admit it, I know I will.

My dad steps forward, uncrossing his arms to place a warm, sweaty palm on each of my forearms. Leaning in, he kisses me on the forehead. "We're so proud of you," he says, his voice thick with emotion.

Avoiding eye contact, my mom squeezes in between us and hugs me tightly, resting her face on my jacket. She whispers, "Have fun. Just promise me you'll be careful."

"I promise," I assure her, though a knot of anxiety twists in my stomach.

As my boarding pass is scanned, a wave of emotions washes over me. I turn to catch one last glimpse of my family: my sister frantically waving, my mom pacing nervously, and my dad rocking back and forth with his hands in his jean pockets. Taking a deep breath, I muster the courage to wave my final goodbye. *There's no turning back now.*

May 15, 1993
Stepping into the Heart of Guayaquíl

I 've finally arrived in Guayaquil, Ecuador, after a long journey with three connecting flights. Standing in the airport, reality hits me, and I'm suddenly overwhelmed with uncertainty. *What was I thinking coming here? What should I do now? Where should I go?* Clutching my carry-on tightly, I take a deep breath and head to the bathroom to collect myself.

Leaving the restroom, a short woman in a black sundress approaches me, tugging at my sleeve. "Señorita…" My mom's words echo in my mind: "Just promise me you'll be careful." Unable to understand her and wary of her intentions, I shrug off the stranger and walk away quickly.

My heart races as I try to put some distance between us. I scan the crowded airport for any signs in English or someone who might be able to help me. Across the room, I spot a guy holding a sign with my name on it, along with two others—Amy Miller and Kate Bennett.

I wish I'd known other girls from the program were on my flight. It would've made the journey way less daunting.

I make my way toward the guy. "Hey, I'm Olivia Weber," I say, pointing to my name on his sign.

His face lights up with a warm smile. "Ah, Señorita Weber! Welcome to Ecuador!" He introduces himself as Señor Rodriguez, the program director.

As we greet him, he surprises me with a warm embrace and air kisses on the cheek. The gesture catches me off guard, but I find it sweet. How nice, I think to myself, already feeling a bit more at ease in this unfamiliar place.

I turn to the other two girls, Amy and Kate, and introduce myself. We exchange nervous smiles, all clearly feeling a mix of excitement and apprehension about the adventure ahead.

"Ladies, shall we grab your luggage?" Señor Rodriguez asks, gesturing toward the baggage claim area. As we follow him, I feel a sense of relief and growing anticipation. *This is really happening. I'm in Ecuador, and my study abroad experience is about to begin.*

"Olivia?" The woman who tried to get my attention earlier steps forward, and Señor Lopez introduces her as my host mother, Ramona. Stunned and embarrassed by my earlier actions, my whole body starts to shake. *Oh no, what have I done?*

Ramona leans in to give me a hug and kisses me on the cheek. "Mucho gusto."

Where are my manners? "Sí, mucho gusto," I manage through nervous laughter.

Ramona takes my hand and leads me outside to a van where a man and two small kids are waiting. Unlike his wife, Victor looks just like the black-and-white photo I got in the mail. But in the picture, he looked so serious—squinting, with furrowed brows, a creased forehead, and pursed lips. Today, he's all smiles.

I reach out to shake Victor's hand. Instead, he invites me into a hug, and I gladly accept the gesture. *Everyone is so friendly.*

While Victor puts my luggage in the back of the van, Ramona encourages the kids to say hi. Cristina, almost as tall as her mom, with dark, shoulder-length hair, introduces herself first. Enrique, who's only up to his mom's waist, looks a little shy.

"Adelante," Ramona encourages.

Peeking from behind his mom's leg, the toddler—mop of dark hair and big brown eyes—waves with a quick, bashful grin. "Hi."

My eyes are drawn to Ramona's midsection, and I finally understand why she looks so different from her profile picture; her face is fuller, but most noticeably, she has a small baby bump just visible beneath the loose fabric of her sundress.

Despite my initial embarrassment, I start to feel a warm acceptance from my new host family. This is the beginning of my adventure in Ecuador, and I'm ready to embrace it.

As Victor navigates through the crowded airport parking lot, he pops a tape into the cassette player. I instantly recognize the opening notes of "Stand by Me" by Ben E. King. A smile spreads across my face as I listen to him sing along in broken English, effortlessly hitting every note. I close my eyes, savoring the moment.

Suddenly, my body jerks forward as Victor accelerates across four lanes of traffic to make a sharp left into the busy street. Loud rhythms and honking horns drown out the familiar ballad. Trying to regain my balance, I grip my seat tightly. *Thank goodness I'm wearing a seatbelt.*

Victor stays in the left lane, closely following the car in front of him, while more aggressive drivers weave in and out of traffic. A guy on a motorcycle zooms up onto the sidewalk to dodge a row of parked cars. Other motorists run red lights, change lanes without signaling, and speed like it's a race. Completely overwhelmed by all the sights and sounds, I wonder if there are any driving rules here.

Almost an hour later, just after midnight, Victor pulls up to a row of homes on the outskirts of the city and announces, "¡Estamos en casa!"

Cristina translates, "We're home."

In the darkness, I see a row of cement houses with gated courtyards, flat concrete roofs, and metal bars over the doors and windows. I feel a mix of exhaustion and excitement as I take in my new surroundings. The chaotic drive has left me a bit shaken, but the warm welcome from my host family eases my nerves.

As I step into their home, I'm filled with curiosity about what my life will be like here over the coming months. Despite the late hour, I try to stay alert and soak in every detail of my new living space, knowing this moment marks the start of my adventure in Ecuador.

Victor grabs my luggage from the back of the van as Ramona leads me inside. "Nuestra casa es tu casa (Our home is your home)."

"Muchas gracias," I say, feeling grateful and excited for what's ahead in this new home and country.

"Come on!" Cristina tugs on my arm and races up the tile stairs, motioning for me to follow. Smiling wide, she leads me down a short hallway to the guest room. Standing in the doorway, I scan the room—a double bed, shelves on either side, a digital alarm clock, a wall unit with an air conditioner, and a private bathroom with a shower.

Both kids rush past me to the bathroom. Ramona gestures for me to join them, pointing to a trash can beside the toilet. "Don't flush toilet paper," Cristina tells me.

It's been a long day, so Ramona and the kids leave my room, closing the door behind them. I fumble through my suitcase to find a pair of pajamas and my cosmetics; unpacking can wait until tomorrow.

My air-conditioned room felt refreshing when I first arrived, a welcome escape from the heat and humidity outside. But now, the cool air feels a bit too chilly against my skin. Shivering slightly, I crawl under the covers and pull the white, eyelet comforter up to my chin, cocooning myself in its warmth.

I wonder what my friends and family are doing back home. *Do they miss me?* I definitely miss them.

As homesickness tugs at my heart, I will myself to stay positive. *It's gonna be okay,* I think as I drift off to sleep in this strange new place. This is just the beginning of my journey, and I'm determined to make the most of every moment, even as I adjust to this new environment and culture.

May 16, 1993
CONNECTING WITH MY HOST FAMILY

A s the bright red numbers on the digital clock come into focus, I'm stunned by how late it is. Almost noon—no way I slept that long! Rubbing the sleep from my eyes, I stretch my arms and yawn, swinging my legs over the side of the bed. My bare feet hit the cool tile floor. A hot shower would be perfect to shake off the grogginess.

I step into my private bathroom, eager to wash away the sleep and travel grime. But when I turn the faucet handle, I'm met with a disappointing trickle of icy water. No matter how I adjust the knob, the temperature stays the same.

I let the water run for a few minutes, hoping it'll warm up, but the cold spray keeps coming, and I start to shiver. Still determined to rinse off, I detach the showerhead and hold it close to my body, quickly washing each area individually, the cold water stinging my skin.

Bending forward, I wet my hair and lather it with two-in-one shampoo and conditioner, silently thanking my mom for the space-saving idea. As I massage the suds into my scalp, I tilt my head back, trying to keep most of the water from running down my back.

With my damp hair in a messy ponytail, I leave my room and decide to check out the sounds of laughter and chatter coming from down the hall.

Standing in the doorway, I take in the scene. The whole host family is piled together on a huge king-sized bed, their eyes glued to a small TV flickering with cartoon characters. Victor and Ramona are propped against the wooden headboard, pillows scattered behind them, while the kids snuggle between them, giggling at the antics on-screen.

I'm struck by their closeness—there's no concern for personal space. They seem to draw comfort and joy from just being together. It's a stark contrast to what I'm used to, but there's something heartwarming about it.

Cristina is the first to notice me. She hops off the bed and greets me at the door with a bright smile. "Afternoon!"

"Yeah, hey," I reply, a slight blush creeping across my cheeks. "Buenas tardes."

Victor stands up, moving gently to support his pregnant wife, offering his hands to help her find her footing. The tenderness in his actions is touching.

Ramona speaks in Spanish and Cristina translates. "How did you sleep?"

"Ah, muy bien," I say.

"Want something to eat or drink?" Cristina asks.

"No, no gracias," I politely decline.

"Want to call your family?" she offers.

I pause, thinking it over. Nodding yes, Ramona leads me downstairs to a beige push-button phone on a glass stand in their formal living room. Following the prompts on the back of my international calling card, I anxiously wait to see who picks up.

"Hello."

"Hey, Dad."

"Jackie, it's Olivia!" I can hear my dad yelling for my mom. "Honey, it's so good to hear your voice!"

I picture my parents hovering by the wall phone in the kitchen; Mom standing while Dad sits at the table so they both can reach the receiver. Overcome with emotion, I discreetly brush away tears. Can't let them know I'm crying.

"How was your flight?" Dad asks.

"Long, but I sat next to a nice guy named Manuel on the last leg. We talked most of the time."

"Did you sleep at all?" Mom wants to know.

"Not really."

"You must've been wiped by the time you got there," she comments.

"Oh yeah." I had flown from Pennsylvania to New York, then to Raleigh-Durham, and finally to Guayaquil. The last leg of the trip was almost ten hours.

"I bet you crashed hard last night," Dad chuckles.

"I did. Slept until noon."

"What time is it there now?" Mom asks.

"It's almost two o'clock."

Dad processes this and says, "So Ecuador is technically only one hour behind us."

Mom quickly changes the subject. "How's the family?"

"They're so nice. Everyone came to the airport to pick me up. Victor, the dad, played 'Stand by Me' and knew every word, even though he doesn't speak much English. Ramona, the mom, is pregnant. I'm not sure when she's due, but it's gotta be soon. I didn't even recognize her at the airport."

"What about the kids?"

"Enrique is adorable but really shy. Cristina is super friendly and helpful. She speaks English."

"Okay, we better let you go," Dad says. "Don't wanna run out of minutes on your first call home."

"I'll call again next weekend," I promise. Just then, it's time for lunch.

Putting down the receiver, I feel a mix of emotions. Hearing my parents' voices makes me homesick, but I'm also grateful for their support and the warmth of my host family. Taking a deep breath, I head to join everyone for lunch, ready to dive into Ecuadorian food and embrace this new adventure.

Victor sits at the head of the table. Enrique, of course, is next to Ramona; Cristina and I sit directly across from them. Nilda, the housekeeper, prepares servings for everyone.

I survey the plate in front of me—a long, flat piece of steak, a bed of fluffy white rice topped with a fried egg, French fries, fried plantains, and a handful of fresh lettuce leaves with juicy tomatoes, crunchy red onions, cool cucumbers, and a slice of avocado.

"Churrasco," Cristina calls it.

An egg over rice? I watch Cristina break the yolk of her egg and add ketchup to her rice.

"You like?" she offers.

"No, no gracias."

As I bring the fork to my lips, the room falls silent, everyone holding their breath, eager for my reaction to the first bite.

"Ah… muy bien," I say, my voice warm with appreciation.

Victor nods approvingly. With a gentle smile, he turns to the rest of the family and says, "Comer."

I enjoy everything on my plate, especially the fried plantains. I've had them before, but never like this. The crispy edges and caramelized texture give them a sweet taste. They remind me of butterscotch.

After finishing every last bite, I lean back with a contented sigh. Excusing myself from the table, I head back to my room. I gather the gifts I carefully packed for everyone. Though the bows are a bit crushed, each gift is still wrapped in colorful paper.

With a mix of excitement and nervousness, I return to the dining room and hand out the gifts one by one. I watch their faces light up with anticipation as they unwrap the festive paper.

Cristina opens her package first—a five-hundred-piece jigsaw puzzle featuring a scene from *The Little Mermaid.* "Muchas gracias," she beams, hugging the box. She wants to start working on it right away, but Ramona tells her she needs to wait.

Enrique's eyes light up when I hand him a present wrapped in *Teenage Mutant Ninja Turtles* paper. With a nod, he tears it open—it's a one-hundred-piece puzzle from *Aladdin.*

"¡Que lindo!" Ramona and Victor exclaim simultaneously.

"Dile gracias," Ramona encourages him.

In a timid voice, Enrique thanks me for his gift.

"Para ustedes y ustedes," I say, handing Ramona and Victor each their own gift.

Ramona asks Enrique if he wants to help open her package. Together, they peel back the paper to reveal a box of assorted Hershey chocolates.

"Chocolate," Ramona holds the box up for everyone to see.

Enrique quickly tries to pick a piece, with his sister reaching across the table to do the same.

Victor rips the wrapping paper from his gift to reveal a box of saltwater taffy. He carefully unrolls one of the wax wrappers, pausing to examine the long piece of candy. Maybe he's never had taffy.

"Taf-ee," I pronounce clearly.

"Taf-ee," he repeats. Taking a bite of the soft candy, his eyes widen as he tastes it.

"Mmm," he says, smacking his lips. Licking the stickiness from his fingers, he declares it "Que delicioso." Ramona and both kids grab a piece, too.

Watching everyone enjoy their taffy, warmth spreads through my chest. Their genuine excitement and appreciation for these small tokens from my home makes me feel more connected to them. In this moment, despite being far from my own family, I feel a sense of belonging.

"Vamos arriba," Ramona suggests.

Nilda clears the table while the rest of us head back upstairs to the parents' bedroom, Cristina and Enrique bringing their puzzles with them. Cristina asks if they can start on hers, but eventually agrees to begin with Aladdin.

Victor carefully cuts the box open with a pocketknife and empties the pieces onto the tile. Sprawled out on the floor, I join the kids as we start flipping pieces face-up. I look for edges, and they quickly pick up on my strategy and help me. Once we have the frame, we search for pieces with similar colors and designs.

While the kids and I play, Ramona and Victor lay on their bed watching a telenovela. I've never seen a soap opera on a Sunday afternoon. Even without understanding everything, the background music and dramatic acting clearly communicate the story.

"What are your parents' names?" Cristina asks.

"John and Jackie." I quickly correct myself. "Mi madre se llama Jackie y mi padre se llama John."

"Brothers or sisters?"

I tell her I have a younger sister named Beth.

"Pets?"

She finds out I have a cat named Cuddles. Their family has a dog, but it's more for protection than as a pet.

"When's your birthday?"

Mine is January sixth. Coincidentally, Cristina's birthday is in January too—just two days apart.

Chatting with Cristina helps me feel more at ease. I assume she's just as excited to practice her English.

I had a bit of Spanish in middle school; Cristina started learning English in kindergarten. Enrique, who only goes to preschool twice a week, has already been introduced to the alphabet, numbers, and colors at age three.

"What's your favorite color?" Cristina asks.

"Violeta."

Cristina's favorite color is pink.

Enrique jumps in, saying his favorite color is "wellow."

"Yeh-low," I correct, pointing to my mouth.

Still struggling with the 'y', he repeats, "Weh-low."

As he keeps trying to say "yellow," I can't help but smile at his determination.

"Como plátanos," Enrique proudly exclaims, bouncing around the room, arms swinging as he imitates a monkey. "Ooh, ooh, ah, ah!" he hoots, scrunching up his face in an exaggerated monkey expression.

His performance catches us all off guard, and we burst into laughter. Cristina giggles uncontrollably, holding her sides, while I can't help but join in. Even Victor and Ramona pause their telenovela to chuckle at Enrique's antics. His playful imitation reminds me that laughter really is a universal language.

As I reflect on my first day, I write about the time spent with my Ecuadorian host family. I thoroughly enjoyed just hanging out and getting to know them. Honestly, chilling in the parents' bedroom felt a bit intrusive at first, but once I realized it was more like a family room, it felt cozy and inviting.

I think to myself, "I think I'm gonna like it here." The warmth and closeness of this family is different from what I'm used to, but it's starting to feel welcoming. This experience is already teaching me so much about family dynamics in a different culture, and I can't wait to see what else I'll learn during my stay.

May 17, 1993
CLASSROOM CONNECTIONS: MAKING FRIENDS

T he next morning, the alarm clock beeps incessantly, jolting me awake. Today's the big day—my first day of classes at the university! My heart races with a mix of excitement and nerves as I remember the effort I put into preparing for this moment.

Last night, I meticulously ironed every wrinkle from my outfit. I know I only get one chance to make a first impression, and I'm determined to dress for success. I chose mauve rayon dress pants and a matching short-sleeved top, adding a chiffon scarf with black, emerald green, white, and mauve for a pop of color. I finish off the look with black-heeled sandals.

When I head downstairs, I find Ramona at the table, engrossed in a newspaper. "Por favor," she gestures for me to sit. Nilda prepares a plate, setting it in front of me with a smile—scrambled eggs and rice, along with a vibrant fruit salad of papaya, bananas, and pineapple.

Out the window, I spot Enrique zipping around the courtyard in his battery-operated car, while the older woman from last night tends to the laundry. Cristina must have already left for school. Without her there to help translate, I eat in silence, the sounds of laughter and chatter around me feeling distant.

After breakfast, I head back upstairs to use the bathroom. Standing in front of the mirror, I gently rub sunscreen onto my face, blending it over my already-applied makeup. A lump forms in my throat as I catch a glimpse of moisture gathering in the corners of my eyes. What if no one speaks English? The thought sends a wave of anxiety through me.

"Estás lista?" Ramona calls from downstairs.

"Sí," I reply, grabbing my oversized handbag—a mix of purse and backpack—and rushing back down.

As we climb into the family van, a young girl, slightly older than me, joins us.

"Aló! I'm Mayra," she says, her smile warm and inviting.

"Hola. Me llamo Olivia," I respond, feeling a blend of nerves and excitement.

"Nice to meet you," she replies, her Spanish accent thick.

I remember from the application that Ramona drives kids to and from school. As we travel from house to house, Mayra lifts youngsters, all around four or five years old, in and out of the van.

I'm amused by the dozen adorable kids in perfectly pressed uniforms, their chatter filling the vehicle with lively energy. They point at me and whisper, and for the first time, being the center of attention feels wonderful.

After dropping off the last child with his teacher, Mayra returns to the passenger seat and turns to me. "You from the United States?"

"Sí, de Pennsylvania," I reply, grateful for her effort to communicate.

Mayra genuinely engages me in conversation during our fifteen-minute ride to the university. Her warmth helps to calm my nerves, allowing me to relax.

When we arrive at the university, Ramona and Mayra walk me to where the group of exchange students is meeting. I spot Señor Rodriguez energetically waving to me from across the courtyard.

"¡Hola, Olivia!" He greets me with a hug and an air kiss on the cheek. "¿Cómo estás?"

"Muy bien," I respond. In English, I add, "My family is so nice."

He had called our home the previous day to check on me. Even though they've hosted numerous exchange students over the years, he wanted to make sure I was settling in well. I thank him for his kindness.

Señor Rodriguez introduces me to the other six students studying abroad with me: Sharon, Derek, Julia, and Rashad. "Of course, you've met Amy and Kate at the airport," he adds.

"Yeah, we arrived on the same flight," I confirm.

Our diverse group includes Rashad, the oldest, from Egypt; Derek, the youngest, from the Midwest; and the rest of us from various parts of the Northeast. Standing among them, I'm swept up in a wave of excitement. This is the start of an incredible journey, and I'm ready to embrace every moment.

Our morning begins with a tour of the university, and my heart flutters with anticipation. The campus looks small from the outside but boasts massive four-story buildings nestled in the city center. As we walk, our guide informs us, "The elevator is for emergencies only." I mentally prepare myself for a lot of stairs, which makes me both nervous and excited.

He shares a brief history lesson: "Universidad Laica de Vicente Rocafuerte is named after a prominent Guayaquil resident who served as Ecuador's president from 1834 to 1839. He completed his education in Madrid, Spain." He adds, "The university prides itself on educating the working class, offering convenient schedules—including evening classes—to accommodate work hours." I feel a surge of admiration for the institution's commitment to accessibility.

Our schedule includes morning sessions with two classes alongside Ecuadorian students, focusing on Ecuador's history and culture. "From 1 PM to 3 PM, we observe the traditional 'siesta'—a break from the intense heat to spend time with family or even nap after the day's main meal," our guide explains. The idea of midday naps fills me with comfort and relief.

On our first day, the college hosts a warm welcome, gifting us with memorabilia—a pennant, a t-shirt, a padfolio, pens, pencils, and folders. Faculty from various departments greet us enthusiastically, and I feel a rush of belonging.

During our free time between lunch and the evening session, I chat with my new classmates about our living arrangements.

"What's your place like?" Amy asks.

"Tiny," Kate replies. "I think my bedroom here is about the size of my closet back home."

Sharon shares, "I'm staying with an elderly woman in her apartment. It's noisy, but that's city living for you."

"What about you, Olivia?" Amy inquires.

"I actually live outside the city," I say.

Sharon follows up, "What are the homes like there?"

"They're row homes with gated patios, metal bars on the doors and windows. Most are dark beige with white trim," I giggle. "I could easily get confused about which house I live in, since they all look the same."

"So, what's the house like?" Kate asks.

"It's cute. I have my own bedroom and a private bath."

"Are you kidding?" Amy interjects. "I'm one of nine people living under the same roof, and we only have one bathroom to share."

I decide not to mention that my host family has three bathrooms, or to elaborate further on my other accommodations.

"Speaking of bathrooms," Kate says, "why don't they flush toilet paper?"

"I read that most places in Ecuador don't have adequate plumbing," Sharon explains. "If you flush toilet paper, it could cause a clog."

"Well, if they don't empty the garbage in the bathroom soon, I think I might barf," Amy announces to the group.

"You girls know not to drink the water, right?" Sharon adds.

"I bought a case of water as soon as I got here," Amy says, raising a plastic bottle of purified water.

"What's that on your arm?" I ask Amy.

Sharon gently examines the underside of Amy's forearm. "It looks like some sort of bug bite," she says, rubbing her finger over a raised rash.

"Probably fleas," Amy replies.

"Why do you think that?" Kate asks.

"There was this scrawny stray cat roaming around. I felt bad and fed it. It followed me home, and I snuck it into my room. It wasn't until it was curled up in my bed with me that I started scratching."

"You need to be careful," Sharon warns.

"Yeah, with all the strays out there, how do you know it's not rabid?" Kate comments.

As we share our stories and concerns, I sense a mix of camaraderie and unease. I hesitate to reveal too much about my own situation.

Our evening classes focus on Spanish language instruction, tailored to individual proficiency levels. Despite four years of high school Spanish and a college semester, I'm still classified as a beginner.

Derek and I are the only students in our group, and the intimacy of the small class makes me acutely aware of my shortcomings. Our professor, though kind and patient, sets high standards and assigns daily homework. As a people-pleaser, I know I'll need to study hard to meet his expectations—especially in such a small class where there's no room to hide.

After class, a wave of relief washes over me as I find Ramona and Mayra waiting for me, just as they promised. Their reliability brings a sense of security in this unfamiliar environment. Once home, I'm served a bowl of soup, and I remember that Victor works away during the week. Everyone else has already eaten; the kids are bathed and in bed, leaving the house in serene quietness.

Retreating to my room, I can't believe how much my feet ache. Red marks crisscross the tops, and painful blisters have formed on my heels. Wincing as I examine them, I resolve to wear open-backed sandals tomorrow to spare my feet further discomfort.

I settle in to write in my journal, reflecting on the day's experiences. As I jot down my thoughts, I realize I've learned some valuable lessons. Along with the discomfort of swollen feet in this humid climate, I've discovered that certain fabrics can be unforgiving. I mentally note that rayon, with its tendency to wrinkle, might not be the best choice for my wardrobe after all.

Reflecting on my first day, I feel a deep sense of gratitude for my host family arrangement. Compared to the experiences shared by my fellow students, my situation seems almost luxurious. I have my own bedroom with air conditioning and a private bathroom— amenities that none of the others enjoy. The presence of caretakers, maids, and nannies in my host family's home is another stark contrast to the other students' accommodations.

While Ramona drives me to and from school, the others must navigate the city independently. Their living situations seem more basic—they're provided with meals, though apparently not as elaborate as mine, and a place to sleep. They handle their own laundry and transportation, tasks I'm spared from managing.

As I prepare for bed, I feel a mix of excitement for the experiences ahead and gratitude for the comforts I've been afforded in my host family's home. Despite the challenges, I am filled with anticipation for the journey that lies ahead, eager to embrace each moment and grow from this incredible opportunity.

May 20, 1993
CURIOSITY AND CONNECTION

"Gringa," they call me. It's a label that sticks with me everywhere I go in this new place, a constant reminder that I'm an outsider. At first, it felt jarring, almost like a sting, but over time, I've grown used to it. It's become part of my identity as I navigate this unfamiliar world.

I can't help but draw attention. People greet me wherever I go, like I've got some kind of celebrity status, though I'm far from famous back home. It's flattering, but sometimes it's a bit much. I find myself constantly in the spotlight, a curiosity to be checked out and chatted up.

My appearance sets me apart, even when I try to blend in. My skin, darkening each day under the relentless sun, is still lighter than most of the locals'. My hair, which I've always thought was just wavy, fascinates my new friends with its beautiful curls. They touch it, comment on it, marvel at its texture.

And then there's my height. Back home, at five feet, three inches tall, I was pretty average. Here, I feel like a giant. My thicker bone structure makes me tower over the petite women around me. I find myself looking down more often than not, guessing that the average height here must be less than five feet.

Being so noticeable is a strange feeling. Every day is a balancing act of embracing my uniqueness while wishing I could just fit in. But with each passing day and new interaction, I'm learning to carry this "gringa" label with some grace. It's not just about how they see me, but how I choose to see myself in this vibrant, unfamiliar world.

Another thing that sets me apart is my Spanish. As I try to communicate, people patiently listen and help me out. Navigating conversations in a language I'm still learning is both challenging and rewarding.

There's a twist to these interactions, though. As soon as people realize I speak English, a lot of them get super eager to practice their English instead of letting me speak Spanish.

It's a bit of a double-edged sword. On one hand, I'm flattered by their interest and happy to help. On the other, I sometimes feel a little disappointed because I wanted to dive deep into Spanish.

After class, I decide to stick around and chat with one of my professors, telling my friends I'll meet them at the mall for lunch. Afterward, I walk to the curb of the busy street where people are hailing cabs. "¿Cualquiera que vaya al Policentro?" I stammer to a crowd, hoping someone understands my broken Spanish.

"Sí," says one of the girls. "Come with me." Someone else in a van waves me over. "Let's go," the girl says, grabbing my hand.

I hesitate, glancing at the packed van. "¿Estas segura?" I ask, making sure there's enough room.

"Sí, sí," several passengers say, clearing a space for two more.

Sandwiched between strangers, I'm jostled around as the driver weaves in and out of traffic. I silently pray, "Just let me make it there alive."

"Where you from?" the girl asks.

"Los Estados Unidos (The United States)," I reply.

She introduces herself as Perla and tells me she thought I might be an American studying at the university. She's excited to share that she's a student there too and works at one of the department stores, so she's on her way to work.

Perla and I hop out at the mall, walk together to her store, and chat for almost an hour.

I glance down at my watch, surprised at how easily we lost track of time. "I'm so sorry," I say.

"Why?" she asks.

"I made you late."

"No worries," she reassures me with a smile.

Used to the fast-paced life back in Pennsylvania, I can't help but feel anxious. But Perla doesn't seem bothered at all. Instead, she introduces me to her boss, and we end up chatting for another hour.

By the time I get to the food court, my friends are wrapping up and getting ready to head back to campus. "What took you so long?" Sharon asks.

"I met this sweet girl named Perla, and we totally lost track of time," I explain.

"We were starting to worry," Amy adds.

"Hey, at least everything's cool now," Kate interjects.

In this whirlwind of new experiences and connections, I'm not just learning about a new culture but also about the kindness and patience of strangers who quickly become friends.

The Ecuadorian who intrigues me the most is Mayra, and I'm equally captivated by her. Each evening, after dinner, we retreat to my air-conditioned room to study together. Having someone to practice my Spanish with is a joy, and Mayra genuinely loves helping me expand my conversational skills. She also gets to practice her English with me, which seems to delight her. I feel comfortable making mistakes around her, and I welcome her constructive criticism. I crave honest feedback, and Mayra doesn't hold back.

Curious about Ramona's pregnancy, I ask Mayra, "¿Cuándo Ramona tiene un bebé?"

"Ella está embarazada," Mayra corrects me.

"She's embarrassed?" I say, confusion washing over me.

"Dice 'está embarazada,'" she repeats.

In that moment, I realize there isn't a direct translation from English to Spanish. A wave of relief washes over me that I never tried to tell someone I was embarrassed, as they might have thought I meant I was pregnant!

"Dará a luz a finales del próximo mes," Mayra tells me, her eyes sparkling with excitement. (She'll give birth at the end of next month.)

I can hardly contain my joy at the thought of being here when the baby arrives!

Eager to learn more about Mayra and her relationship with Ramona, I ask, "¿Quién es Ramona para ti (Who is Ramona to you)?"

Unsure of the English translation, Mayra tells me, "Era mi faro de luz."

I tilt my head, trying to process her words. *A lighthouse?* How can a person be considered a lighthouse? Intrigued by her description, I'm eager to understand more about their bond.

"Wanna know about me?" Mayra asks.

"Sí," I reply eagerly.

Even though Mayra is only two years older than me, she seems much older; the lines on her face and the creases around her eyes suggest a painful past. If she's open to sharing, I want to know all I can about my new friend. We sit facing each other on my bed, and I give Mayra my full attention.

I learn that Mayra grew up about one hundred twenty-five miles from Guayaquíl, in the countryside of coastal Ecuador. She's the oldest of five kids, with four younger brothers, and was born into abject poverty. Families in Mayra's village didn't have running water, let alone clean drinking water.

I've read about situations like this, but until it affects someone you know, it's just a story. I ask Mayra where they got water to drink and how they washed their clothes.

She explains that rivers, small bodies of water, and even puddles after rain were their water sources. They used the same polluted water for drinking, washing clothes, and bathing.

Mayra describes her family's home: a one-room dilapidated shack with a straw roof and a dirt floor. No electricity, no furniture. They ate and slept on that same dirt floor. Food was scarce, and there were many days Mayra went hungry.

A pang of guilt washes over me for the comforts I've always taken for granted. The stark contrast between our upbringings leaves me feeling both humbled and deeply saddened.

When Mayra was twelve, she went to live with her aunt, who worked as a housekeeper for a family in the city. Her aunt had asked her employers to take in Mayra in exchange for her help with cleaning, while her parents received a monthly allowance.

As Mayra continues recounting her move to the city, I find myself leaning in, captivated by her story. I can see the excitement dancing in her eyes as she describes the wonders of her new home—running water, electricity, a real bed. My heart swells with a bittersweet mix of joy for her newfound comforts and sorrow for the deprivation she had known.

But when Mayra looks me directly in the eye and confides, "Mi jefe me violó muchas veces (My boss raped me many times)," my world seems to stop spinning. The horror of her words hits me like a physical blow.

I feel nauseous, my mind reeling as I struggle to process what she is telling me. Tears prick at my eyes as Mayra recounts the repeated abuse, her voice steady but her pain palpable.

Rather than try to help her escape, the jealous wife was intent on punishing her. One evening, in a fit of drunken rage, she beat Mayra with a belt and pulled clumps of hair out of her head. This was the beginning of many attempts to hurt her, but by this point, Mayra was numb to pain and had learned how to mask the emotional trauma trapped within her existence.

As she describes the wife's jealous rage and physical abuse, I instinctively reach out to rub Mayra's arm, desperate to offer some comfort, however small. My heart breaks for the young girl she was, trapped in a nightmare with no escape.

Mayra kept the secrets of physical and sexual abuse from her aunt and the rest of her family. Whether her aunt didn't see the welts from physical abuse or simply chose to ignore the scars, it was just a part of life Mayra had come to expect and accept.

As I listen to Mayra's story, a whirlwind of emotions washes over me. My heart aches with every word she speaks, each revelation more shocking than the last.

"But then…" Mayra pauses, her expression softening. She lights up as she recalls the day she met Ramona. Mayra had been sent out, barefoot and barely clothed, to buy bananas. Coincidentally, Ramona and Enrique were shopping at the same corner market.

When Mayra's story shifts to her meeting with Ramona, I feel a surge of hope and gratitude. Ramona asked Mayra if she was okay. Unsure how to respond and not knowing if the woman would help or hurt her, Mayra just bowed her head and whispered, "Yeah."

Over the next few weeks, Mayra and Ramona ran into each other all the time. Ramona invited Mayra to live with her and work for her. Mayra barely knew Ramona, but it had to be better than her current situation. It wasn't really her choice, though, so she told

Ramona she needed to talk to her current employers and her parents first.

Even though there was no official paper formalizing the agreement, Ramona basically adopted Mayra. More importantly, she rescued her from years of suffering, giving her a reason not just to live, but to thrive.

I now get why Mayra described Ramona as a lighthouse—she truly was Mayra's 'Beacon of Light.'

After our conversation, I write about Mayra's heartbreaking story in my journal. Retelling it is emotionally draining and mentally exhausting. I can't even begin to imagine living through such experiences.

As I toss and turn in bed, I think about Ramona. I was already fond of her, but now I see her in a whole new light. I feel so grateful to be sharing this experience under her roof. I realize how lucky I am to be with this family, witnessing firsthand the profound impact of compassion and kindness.

May 24, 1993
LOVE AT FIRST SIGHT

O n Monday morning, Amy arrives to class buzzing with excitement. She just went to a barbeque with her host sister, Elena, and met the most amazing people. Her eyes are sparkling as she raves about one guy in particular, admitting she's totally crushing on him.

His name is Javier, a local merchant who sells goods at La Bahía, an open market by the bay. He invited her to check out his stall, and she pulls out a crumpled piece of notebook paper with the location scribbled on it. "You guys, you've gotta come with me during siesta to meet him!" she pleads.

Derek rolls his eyes. "I don't think that's a good idea."

Julia chimes in, cautious as always. "Señor Rodriguez warned us not to visit places he hasn't pre-approved, especially with all the crime around. Tourists shouldn't go to unfamiliar spots without a buddy."

Her reminder hits home; she's not wrong. We stand out, and that makes us targets in unknown areas.

Everyone pauses, weighing Amy's excitement against the risks. It's a classic moment of wanting adventure but needing to stay safe in a foreign city.

"Please, come with me!" Amy begs, her enthusiasm infectious.

"Count me in!" Kate says, always up for a wild time.

This leaves Sharon and me. We're hesitant, but we can't let Kate and Amy go alone. Plus, we convince ourselves that it'll be safer as a group. As soon as our morning classes end, we grab a taxi and head to La Bahía.

As we drive, I feel a mix of thrill and nerves. I'm excited to explore and soak up the local culture, but the worry about potential dangers lingers. I remind myself we're in this together, but I make a mental note to stay sharp and keep my stuff close. This could be just the adventure we need, but I hope we're not being too reckless.

When we arrive, doubt starts creeping in. I want to jump back in the taxi and head to the university or ask the driver to take me to Policentro, the local mall. Those places feel safe.

But as I stand there, I can't help but be amazed. I've never seen anything like this. The market stretches endlessly, with rows of stalls offering everything from electronics to home goods, toys, fragrances, cassette tapes, seasonal flowers, jewelry, and clothing. It feels like a treasure trove.

The clothes on display are all over the place— swimwear, streetwear, sports gear, business casual, even stuff for fancy events. There are colorful ethnic pieces like loose guayabera shirts for guys, embroidered blouses for girls, ponchos, vibrant skirts, and traditional shawls. And designer labels like Guess, Calvin Klein, and Ralph Lauren are mixed in too.

The shoe stalls are just as varied, creating a maze of choices that can easily confuse anyone. The market's affordability attracts a mix of people from all walks of life.

The crowd is overwhelming. I keep bumping into folks or getting jostled around. Until now, my travels have been friendly, but this crowd feels different. The locals look annoyed at my clumsiness, giving me judgmental glares.

The afternoon heat is intense, which is why my friends and I usually chill at the air-conditioned mall. Some vendors have fans, but they just blow hot air around. The mix of sweat and different body odors creates a unique, often overpowering scent.

The noise is crazy too. Each stall blasts a different kind of music, drowning out everything else. Conversations turn into shouts, as people have to raise their voices just to hear each other.

Amidst the hustle and bustle, our group huddles together while Amy tries to figure out where we are without asking anyone for help.

"Wah wah, wah wah."

Even though they're speaking English, I can't make out a word. The noise is so loud I can't even think straight. Panic grips me as I fight back tears, just hoping we can get out of here in one piece.

Then, out of the corner of my eye, I spot someone hugging Amy. Relief washes over me—thank goodness we've found Javier's stall!

One by one, Amy introduces us, and we exchange warm hugs and air kisses with Javier.

"Mucho gusto (Nice to meet you)!" Sharon says, smiling at him.

"Mucho gusto," he replies with a grin.

Kate jumps in, "Mucho gusto," and Javier responds, "Encantado de conocerte (Pleased to meet you)."

When it's my turn, I feel butterflies in my stomach. Javier's striking features leave me speechless. He's slightly taller than me, with big brown eyes framed by long lashes and thick dark brows. His bronzed skin and youthful grin shine, contrasting with a faint, mature mustache. Tall, dark, and handsome doesn't even cover it.

"Mucho gusto," I manage to whisper.

"Es un placer (It's a pleasure)," he says, his warm smile making my heart race.

As we hug, I sense something special about this moment. Our eyes lock for a brief second, and I realize Javier was totally worth the risk of coming here.

After some small talk about our stay in Guayaquil, Javier gestures for us to join him in the center of his lively stall. With all the excitement of a sportscaster, he announces, "¡Presento mis amigas americanas (I present my American friends)!"

"Vamos a bailar (We should go dancing)!" he suggests, eager to get us moving.

Sharon immediately shakes her head. As someone who escaped an abusive relationship, she's here to learn the language and soak up the culture, not to party.

But Kate's eyes light up. She can't wait to meet some boys, and Amy is practically glowing at the chance to spend more time with her crush. Unsure of what to say, but not wanting to look like a coward, I reluctantly agree to join them at the disco.

That night, I share the news about Javier with Mayra, knowing she probably doesn't know him. She's thrilled that I've met a guy named Javier who I think is super cute. Sensing my crush, she corrects me: "Tú necesitas decir que él es guapísimo (You need to say that he is extremely handsome; hot)."

May 25, 1993
Salsa Fundamentals:
Learning the Basic Steps

I desperately need to focus on my schoolwork, but studying for my upcoming exam feels like an insurmountable task. The thought of memorizing new vocabulary and perfecting verb conjugations leaves me uninspired. Instead, my mind drifts to dancing, and I bombard Mayra with questions, eager to learn.

In high school, my friends used to tease me at dances. To mask my lack of coordination, I would sway back and forth, moving my left foot to meet my right foot, then stepping back to my original position and shuffling my right foot to meet my left. But if Javier is going to be there, I need to look somewhat sensible.

Mayra tells me salsa and merengue are the dances of choice in Ecuador. I've never heard of these dances, let alone seen anyone perform them. How in the world am I going to pull this off? Panic-stricken, I beg Mayra to be my teacher. "Por favor, enséñame (Please, teach me)," I plead.

Mayra leaves the room and returns shortly thereafter, grinning from ear to ear with a portable cassette player in hand. As she gently places a cassette in the tape deck, she eagerly announces, "Presento a Celia Cruz y salsa."

As soon as she presses play, the room fills with the vibrant sounds of brass and percussion. Mayra clears some space and walks over to me. She leans in, whispering as if sharing a secret, "Salsa es en el ritmo (Salsa is in the rhythm)."

Pulling me off the bed, Mayra starts clapping her hands, encouraging me to join her in finding the beat. "Uno, dos, tres, cuatro (one, two, three, four); cinco, seis, siete, ocho (five, six, seven, eight)." In no time, we are clapping and counting in unison.

As I continue to clap the eight-beat rhythm, Mayra walks me through the basic steps. She demonstrates the footwork, starting with both feet positioned side by side. Slowly and systematically, she shows me how to position my feet on each beat.

On beat one, we step forward with our left foot. For beat two, we step in place with our right foot. On beat three, we bring our left foot back to the neutral position, and on beat four, we pause. After repeating the steps once more, she encourages me to try it on my own.

"Sí, muy bien," Mayra says, her voice filled with warmth.

Building on the sequence, Mayra demonstrates the first four steps again before adding the next four. I try to follow along. On beat five, we step backward with our right foot. Beat six involves stepping in place with our left foot. For beat seven, we bring our right foot back to the neutral position. Once more, beat eight is a pause.

Individually, I find the steps relatively easy to follow. Putting it all together, however, requires more practice and prompting.

"You wanna learn merengue?" Mayra asks, her eyes sparkling with excitement.

Of course, I'm anxious to learn this dance too, but it might be too much for one night.

"How about tomorrow?" I suggest, feeling a mix of exhaustion and eagerness.

"Hasta mañana." Mayra agrees with a smile.

In that moment, I feel a rush of gratitude for Mayra's patience and the joy of learning something new. Despite the challenges, I'm excited to embrace this new cultural experience and dance with confidence.

I take a quick shower before going to bed, the cool water soothing my skin and washing away the perspiration of the day. In my journal, I jot down three reminders: (1) Listen to the music and find the rhythm; (2) Move your hips; (3) Keep your feet on the floor. A smile spreads across my face as I place it next to my alarm clock. I realize there will be no studying tonight, but in the grand scheme of things, it feels like a small sacrifice. Maybe now I won't look foolish and make a complete spectacle of myself in front of Javier and his friends.

Within minutes of laying my head on the pillow, I'm fast asleep, my mind swirling with thoughts of salsa.

May 26, 1993
PARTNERING UP:
THE DYNAMICS OF MERENGUE

I retreat to my room right after dinner, filled with excitement for another dance lesson like the night before. Mayra joins me shortly, bringing music, and we're both eager to continue where we left off. She seems impressed with how well I've retained the salsa steps.

"Ready to learn merengue?" she asks, her eyes sparkling with enthusiasm.

"Sí," I nod, my heart racing.

"Presento Juan Luis Guerra y merengue," Mayra announces, pressing play on the cassette player.

As the music fills the room, I listen intently, noting a slower tempo accompanied by the sounds of guitar, drums, and accordion. Mayra explains that for merengue, I should keep my feet flat on the floor. She demonstrates the basic step, which reminds me of climbing stairs.

Following her lead, I step forward with my left foot, my hip moving to the right. Then I step forward with my right foot, my hip shifting to the left.

Mayra and I take our positions as partners. She places her right hand on my waist and instructs me to rest my left hand on her shoulder. Our opposite hands clasp together, creating a slight space of resistance between us. Before we start moving, Mayra carefully positions my foot between hers to prevent our knees from knocking while we dance.

Standing still, Mayra encourages me to feel the music as we sway our hips to the rhythm. We practice moving across our imaginary dance floor, with Mayra walking forward and me stepping back. After reaching the end, we turn together and repeat the same steps in the opposite direction.

With curiosity, Mayra wants to know more about Javier.

I describe his dark hair and deep brown eyes, realizing this description fits many Ecuadorian men. Still, Mayra listens with sincere interest.

"Tiene una sonrisa hermosa, con (He has a beautiful smile, with) ..." I pause, searching for the right word. "¿Cómo se dice 'dimples'?"

I reach for my Spanish-English dictionary in my schoolbag. As I flip through the pages, Mayra looks over my shoulder, eager to help me find the right word to complete my description of Javier's charming smile.

Scanning the page with my finger, I finally locate the word. Forgetting that the 'h' is silent in Spanish, I start sounding it out, "/h/-/o/-/y/." Mayra immediately interrupts, laughing, and repeats the word correctly for me: "o-yue-los."

Her laughter is infectious, and I can't help but join in, feeling warmth spread through me as we share this moment. The connection we're building feels special, and I'm grateful for her patience and encouragement.

Mayra envelops me in a warm embrace, her excitement evident. With her arms wide open, she exclaims, "I have news!"

She shares that after putting Enrique down for a nap, she gave Ramona, her pregnant patron, a foot rub. During this time, Mayra talked to Ramona about me.

Ramona already knew about my plans to go out with friends on Friday night and had encouraged me to do so. Mayra mentioned that she's been teaching me how to dance and suggested that she and Victor take me to a discoteca. This would let me observe salsa and merengue firsthand, and maybe even practice my new moves.

Ramona was thrilled about the idea of taking me out, introducing me to their friends and sharing more of their culture. Coincidentally, Victor is scheduled to return home a day earlier than usual. She needs to run the idea by him but is confident he'll agree.

I'm beyond excited to hear this great news. "Will you go too?" I ask Mayra, hoping she'll join us.

"No," she tells me, a hint of regret in her voice. "I have work to do."

I feel a pang of sadness that she won't be joining us, but I don't want to pry. Instead, I invite Mayra to help me go through my closet. Together, we select a blue floral dress for the occasion, and I can't help but feel a flutter of anticipation for the night ahead.

May 27, 1993
BUILDING CONFIDENCE ON THE DANCE FLOOR

Exams were scheduled for today, so I arrive home from school a bit early, feeling a mix of relief and anticipation. Victor is already there, and as expected, he's excited about going out tonight. Being away from his beautiful wife all week, especially knowing she's in the final stages of her pregnancy, has been tough. They could both use a night out to unwind and enjoy each other's company.

I thank Ramona and Victor for giving me this chance, my heart swelling with gratitude, and then hurry upstairs to get ready.

At this point in my stay, makeup feels unnecessary. The heat and humidity make my mascara smear, and sweat leaves my face looking oily. Plus, with a clear complexion now golden-brown from the sun, I don't need liquid foundation or blush. Just a bit of lip gloss will do.

After freshening up with a cold compress, I change into the floral dress Mayra helped me pick out the night before. I style my hair with a touch of gel to complete the look, feeling a flutter of excitement in my chest. Tonight promises to be unforgettable, and I can't wait to immerse myself in the vibrant culture and dance the night away.

As I descend the staircase, I find my host parents waiting for me in the formal living room, seated on a plastic-covered white sofa. Victor stands up as I approach, extending his hand to help me with the last step. In a gesture straight out of a fairytale, he gently kisses my hand, then blows me a kiss and exclaims, "Ay, mi gordita!"

The playful moment quickly fades as I process his words. *Gordita?* My mind races—'gordo' means 'fat' in English, and the suffix '–ita' usually means 'small.' *Is he calling me a little fatty?*

My expression must reveal my confusion and discomfort, as my host parents quickly sense they've inadvertently offended me. Ramona calls Cristina downstairs to explain that Victor is actually complimenting me. In their culture, 'gordita' is a term of endearment meaning 'chubby.'

While 'chubby' might sound less offensive, neither word feels particularly flattering to me. Still, determined to smooth over the misunderstanding and make the best of it, I force a smile, trying to embrace the cultural nuance and appreciate the warmth behind the words.

Victor helps his wife climb into the passenger seat of the van, his touch tender and caring, before assisting me with the steep step into the back seat. As we drive toward the city center, music plays through the speakers, weaving a tapestry of sound that mixes with the heavy traffic. Though I don't know the musicians, the style is unmistakable.

"¿Es salsa?" I ask, my voice laced with curiosity.

"Sí, muy bien," they respond, their smiles warm and encouraging.

Before heading to the discoteca, Ramona and Victor stop at Pizza Hut for a quick bite. I'm intrigued by the global fast-food chain; pizza in Ecuador is a delightful surprise, completely different from what I'm used to. With no red sauce on the thick crust, it resembles toasted garlic bread topped with cheese and fresh spices. Yet, like everything I've tasted in Ecuador so far, it's delicious.

Having never been to a nightclub in the U.S., I'm unsure of what to expect. As we pull into a dusty parking lot, I'm surprised to see a relatively small concrete building in the middle of the area. With so many cars parked outside, I wonder how everyone will fit inside.

From the moment I enter, I'm immediately intimidated by the loud music, bright lights, and crowded dance floor. Most of the men are in jeans, t-shirts, and sneakers, while the women wear casual skirts and dresses. Thank goodness I have this experience as a preview to prepare me for my big night.

Across the room, a group waves Victor and Ramona over to join them at their table in the corner of the crowded space. I'm introduced to three other couples, all friends of Victor and Ramona.

"Mucho gusto," followed by warm hugs, are among the exchanged pleasantries.

Unable to converse much because of the loud music, I'm perfectly content to sit silently and watch the couples dance. After all, this is my main goal for the evening.

I love watching Victor and Ramona dance. There's something so sweet about how they hold hands and gaze into each other's eyes. And Ramona, with her large belly, is particularly adorable as she sways to the rhythm like a little penguin.

Looking visibly tired, Ramona returns to the table to take a break. Victor then invites me to switch places with his lovely wife. I happily accept his invitation to be his new partner and nervously join him on the dance floor.

Victor, a natural dancer, serenades me with the lyrics of each song. I'm thankful for Mayra's lessons on the basic dance steps. Despite the practice, I still move awkwardly around the dance floor with some hesitation.

After a fun-filled evening, my heart is full of gratitude. Thanks to Mayra, Victor, and Ramona, I now know what to expect. As I drift off to sleep in the backseat on the way home, I picture myself gliding around the dance floor with grace and confidence. Subconsciously, I just hope I don't step on anyone's toes or fall flat on my face.

May 28, 1993
DRAWN TO EACH OTHER

After our evening class, Amy, Kate, and I rush home, buzzing with excitement for our big night out. As the furgoneta pulls up in front of my host family's residence, I spot Mayra anxiously waiting for me, her energy infectious.

Stepping out of the shower, I see a perfectly pressed floral green and white dress and black open-toed sandals, just waiting for me to slip into.

Mayra helps with my hair and makeup, pulling my hair back on both sides with a barrette at the top of my head, letting my curls cascade just past my shoulders. A subtle touch of lipstick and a glossy sheen complete the look, making me feel both pretty and nervous.

I glance at the digital alarm clock on the shelf beside my bed, my heart racing as it approaches eight-thirty. It's time to go, or I'll be late meeting Amy and Kate.

Ramona offers to have Nilda prepare something small for me to eat. "Quizás un plato de sopa?" she suggests. I respectfully decline, feeling a swarm of butterflies in my stomach. I don't need anything to make my uneasiness worse.

As the van pulls away, Mayra waves at me, her wink and nods full of encouragement, filling me with confidence for the evening ahead. I can feel her support wrapped around me like a warm embrace, bolstering my spirits as I prepare to step into the unknown. The anticipation of the night is a mix of excitement and nerves, and I take a breath, ready to embrace whatever comes next.

Almost simultaneously, Amy's cab and the van driven by Ramona pull into the parking lot. Knowing I'll be home late, Ramona hands me an extra key to their home and tells me to have a good time. I express my gratitude with a heartfelt embrace and a cheerful kiss on the cheek.

As I slide out of my seat in the van, Amy is paying her driver. Now standing side by side, we share a similar unassuming style, while Kate, on the other hand, is sure to make a statement. We sit on a nearby bench, anticipation buzzing in the air.

Fashionably late as usual, Kate makes her grand entrance almost thirty minutes later. Stepping out of her cab, she turns heads, her outfit daring and bold. Amy and I exchange incredulous glances as we take in Kate's sassy style – a short, navy plaid pleated skirt that barely covers her thighs, paired with a white cropped top that accentuates her curves, and black high-heeled sandals with an ankle strap.

Standing under the glow of a streetlamp, I check my watch and notice it's almost ten o'clock. Though we're only a few blocks from the address Javier gave us, the last thing Amy wants to do is keep him waiting. Excitement and nerves swirl within me as I prepare for the night ahead, eager to dance and dive into this vibrant culture.

As soon as we turn the corner, Amy and I spot Javier standing in line outside the nightclub. He looks effortlessly stylish in brown pleated dress pants and a perfectly pressed white long-sleeved shirt, neatly tucked into his belted waistband, with shiny brown loafers completing the look. His dark, short hair is slicked back, adding to his polished appearance. The top three buttons of his Oxford shirt are undone, revealing a gold chain necklace; a gold crucifix ring adorns his right hand.

The moment Javier sees us, he steps out of line and eagerly runs up to us. Amy is the first to receive a warm embrace and a kiss on the cheek. After all, it was through her that we met Javier; without their acquaintance, none of this would be happening right now. The customary hug and air kiss follow as he greets Kate.

But as he approaches me, his cheeky dimples fully exposed and a sparkle in his eye, there's an undeniable attraction. He takes my hands in his and plants a kiss on my cheek.

With his right hand resting on my shoulder, Javier guides Amy, Kate, and me to our place in line. He introduces us to his friend, Mario, who stands casually in black jeans and a blue checkered long-sleeved shirt, paired with sneakers that reflect his laid-back style. Like Javier, Mario shares a similar stature, but his larger bone structure and rounder face give him a different presence. His dark curls are relaxed on top, contrasting with the shaved sides, and he carries an air of shyness that makes him endearing.

Alejandro, on the other hand, clearly needs no formal introduction. He takes Kate's hand and kisses her knuckles with a flourish, exuding confidence. Dressed in white jeans and a black short-sleeved t-shirt with the cuffs rolled up to showcase his bulging biceps, he embodies a casual yet striking appearance. While Javier has an average build, Alejandro is muscular and fit. His edgy haircut, with short sides and dark curls tousled on top, adds to his charm.

There's an undeniable aura of self-assurance about Alejandro, and it's clear he knows how to captivate those around him. As he interacts with Kate, it's evident that he's the perfect match for her—confident, chic, and undeniably charming.

Kate pulls out a cigarette from her handbag and asks for a light, her movements confident and deliberate. She takes a slow, deep inhale, the red-hot embers glowing brightly at the tip, and then seductively exhales, the smoke curling from her pursed lips. As she twists the end of her ponytail, her playful flirtation fills the air, while the rest of us stand in line, engaging in small talk.

"When did you arrive in Ecuador?"

"How long are you staying?"

"What's been your favorite part so far?"

These questions drift around us, blending with the lively atmosphere, but my attention is irresistibly drawn to Javier. He takes care of paying the cover charge and then leads our group to a semi-circular booth in the back of the room.

Alejandro and Kate are the first to arrive, clearly eager to be a couple. Their chemistry is undeniable, and it's clear they're excited to spend the evening together.

I slide in next to Alejandro, letting Amy take the seat next to Kate. Mario positions himself at the end next to Amy, and finally, Javier sits beside me.

As everyone settles in, Javier wanders off. Moments later, he returns to the table, a bottle of rum and six shot glasses in hand. The sight of him sparks a mix of excitement and nerves within me.

As he pours the alcohol into each tiny glass, I start to fidget, bowing my head in embarrassment to avoid making eye contact with anyone. The others eagerly grab their glasses, preparing for a toast, and my heart races at the thought of joining in. I hope I don't look too out of place among them.

Javier tries to hand me the shot he just poured, but he notices my distracted expression. Sensing my hesitation, he leaves the table and heads to the bar. Moments later, he returns with a plastic pitcher of soft drink and two small glasses. With a gentle smile, he offers me a glass of cola, and I gratefully accept.

The camaraderie in the air feels electric, and I can't help but smile, feeling a wave of relief and gratitude toward Javier for making my choice not to drink feel completely accepted. His thoughtful gesture eases my nerves, allowing me to enjoy the moment without any pressure.

As we all raise our glasses, clinking them together and exclaiming, "¡Salud!" I feel a genuine connection with everyone around me, and the warmth of their unspoken support wraps around me like a comforting embrace.

Javier raises his glass, initiating a second toast with just the guys. "¡Quiero hacer un brindis por las americanas (I want to make a toast to the Americans)!" he exclaims, his voice filled with enthusiasm. The energy around the table intensifies as the men prepare to honor Amy, Kate, and me.

As I sip my soda, I watch a third round of shots being poured. Amy and Kate eagerly join in, their excitement palpable. The toast that follows is a lively, spirited affair that captivates my attention.

"¡Arriba!" they shout in unison, raising their glasses high above their heads, the liquid inside catching the light.

"¡Abajo!" comes next, as they lower their glasses dramatically, almost to the table.

"¡Al centro!" they cry, pushing their glasses to the center of the table, clinking them together in a show of camaraderie.

Finally, "¡Adentro!" rings out as they throw back their heads and down the contents of their glasses in one swift gulp.

The energy is infectious, and even though I'm not drinking, I find myself caught up in the moment, grinning at the display of friendship and celebration around me. The warmth of inclusion washes over me, reminding me that I'm part of this group, regardless of what's in my glass.

"¡Ah!" Alejandro exclaims, slamming his glass down on the table, calling for another round. "¡Otra vez!" Only Kate seems willing to keep the momentum going. "Bien hecho," he babbles, laughter erupting between them as they press their foreheads together, giggling like hyenas. "Hehehehe."

"¿Vamos a bailar?" Javier suggests, his eyes twinkling with excitement as he gestures toward the dance floor. He places his hand gently on my back, guiding me to the center of the room. Amy and Mario follow closely behind us, but I can sense a shift in the atmosphere.

As Javier chooses me as his dance partner, I catch a glimpse of disappointment flashing across Amy's face. Knowing about her crush on him, a wave of guilt washes over me. I try to push the feeling aside, but it lingers, creating an invisible barrier between us.

We step onto the dance floor, and I can't help but notice how Amy's smile doesn't quite reach her eyes. Her enthusiasm seems forced, a stark contrast to the genuine excitement she displayed earlier. The realization stings, and I find myself wishing I could somehow ease her feelings without dampening my own joy in this moment.

As the music starts to play, I'm caught between the thrill of dancing with Javier and the nagging awareness of Amy's disappointment. The conflicting emotions swirl within me, creating a bittersweet undercurrent to what should be a carefree night of fun.

The familiar rhythm of salsa fills the air, and despite my hours of practice, I stumble, frantically trying to recall the intricate dance steps. Sensing my unease, Javier signals for me to simply look at him.

"Mírame," he says softly.

I allow him to guide me across the dance floor—if he goes right, I go right; if he speeds up, I speed up. Twists and spins follow, and with each passing second, our connection deepens. Though our moves may not be in sync, Javier's ability to adapt to my missteps touches me profoundly. His constant care and attention in every moment take my breath away. Regardless of how we might look to others, we dance perfectly in each other's eyes, and that's all that matters.

Javier's attention feels intoxicating, and I'm swept up in the thrill of dancing with him, but the weight of Amy's feelings sits heavily on my heart. I want to enjoy this experience, yet I can't shake the feeling that I'm stepping on her toes in more ways than one.

A song called "Meneaito" pumps through the speakers, prompting everyone in the discoteca to rush to the dance floor. The reggae rhythm is unfamiliar, but the group dance is easy to pick up—shuffling right, then left; turning around and doing it again. Hand motions and clapping are incorporated, but the dance is quite simple.

As I try to learn the moves and fall into the rhythm, I'm constantly jostled by others. However, each bump is met with a smile and a nod. The high-energy dance gradually ends, and everyone starts to clap and cheer, "¡Wepa!"

As the applause dies down, so does the tempo of the music, giving way to a romantic ballad. People begin to leave the dance floor, but Javier threads his fingers through mine and pulls me close, wrapping his hands around my waist.

Startled by his affectionate touch, my body stiffens. But as I focus on following his lead, I allow myself to experience the soft flow of the music and relax in his arms. With our bodies almost touching, I feel his warm breath on my cheek and beads of sweat gliding down my face. The fragrant smell of his cologne teases my senses, and the heat between us feels like the haze after rain on a hot, humid day.

Gazing into each other's eyes, I swear he can see into the depths of my soul. A subtle smile forms on my lips as I remind myself that he chose me as his date. Regardless of how or why, I feel like the luckiest girl in the world.

At two o'clock in the morning, the emcee announces the last song of the evening. I find myself longing for more time together, as if I've been watching myself through a dream and need to pinch myself to ensure the last four hours truly happened.

As swarms of people bustle out of the club, Javier and I stay back, scanning the room for our friends. Mario and Amy spent most of the night dancing, while Alejandro and Kate cuddle in a dark corner, getting to know one another a little more intimately.

Having had way too much to drink, Kate leans over and slurs into my ear, "I let his tongue do the talking while his fingers did the walking." I roll my eyes at Kate in disbelief and shake my head. It's quite obvious, as neither one of them can take their hands off each other.

Amy, Kate, and I all met at a park and then walked a few blocks to meet Javier and his friends. It had been prearranged for Javier to drive everyone home, so the six of us pile into his hatchback—Amy and Mario squeeze into the back seat with Alejandro and Kate, while I claim the passenger seat next to Javier.

As soon as we settle in, it becomes clear that Kate and Alejandro have no regard for anyone else in the car. They are wrapped up in each other, kissing and whispering sweet nothings. I feel a mix of embarrassment and disgust at their obliviousness to the rest of us.

As I glance in the rearview mirror, I catch Amy's glare directed at me, her expression a mix of confusion and resentment. I can't tell if she's still upset that Javier chose me over her or if she's simply disgusted by the oblivious behavior of Kate and Alejandro, who are tangled up in their own world next to her.

The atmosphere in the car feels heavy, and I can't shake the feeling of guilt creeping in. I want to enjoy this moment, but Amy's discontent hangs in the air like a storm cloud, casting a shadow over the excitement of the night. It's hard to focus on the laughter and music when I know someone I care about is feeling hurt.

As I attempt to refocus my thoughts, the tension remains unmistakable. My heart pounds rapidly, caught between the exhilaration of Javier's interest and the burden of Amy's emotions. I long to mend the rift, to assure Amy that I never meant to disrupt their relationship, but the opportunity fades as we are obviously not alone. The cheerful laughter from behind us stands in sharp contrast to my inner turmoil.

Javier, sensing the tension, focuses on driving as we make our way through the bustling streets. My home is farthest from the center of the city, so Javier drives me there first. When we pull up to my gated home, he glances at me for confirmation. I hesitate, not wanting this unforgettable evening of music and dancing to ever end, but I reluctantly nod yes.

Javier parks the car and quickly jumps out to open the passenger door for me. As he holds out his hand, helping me from the vehicle, I feel a flutter of excitement. He gently closes the door behind me, and we stand together, loosely holding hands as he gazes deeply into my eyes.

In Spanish, Javier tells me he really likes me. My heart races as I close my eyes, take a deep breath, and whisper back that I like him too.

"Hasta la próxima vez (Until next time)," he says, kissing my forehead softly.

"Hasta luego (Until later)," I reply, my voice barely above a whisper. I quietly open the gate and wave goodbye.

As I place the key in the door, a low growl echoes behind me, jolting me back to reality. I had completely forgotten about the guard dog. In a panic, I push the door open with a force that sends it crashing against the wall, and I rush inside just in time to avoid getting bitten. My heart races as I stand there, trying to catch my breath while the dog barks furiously outside.

Climbing the stairs, I catch a glimpse of Ramona peeking out into the hallway, her expression a mix of concern and curiosity. I quickly apologize for waking her, relief flooding through me when I realize I haven't disturbed anyone else in the house. The warmth of her smile reassures me, but my heart is still pounding from the adrenaline and the unexpected encounter with the dog.

Once in my room, I lean against the door for a moment, letting the events of the night wash over me. The thrill of the evening lingers, but so does the anxiety of being in a new place, where even the simplest things can catch me off guard.

As I undress, I can't shake the thoughts of how late it is. I'm preparing for bed, knowing I'll have to wake up in just a few hours. A quick shower might help me drift off, but I hesitate, not wanting to wash away the lingering scent of Javier. Tossing and turning, I replay the evening in my mind, each moment more vivid than the last.

The night felt almost dreamlike—Javier's gentle touch, his warm smile, the way we moved together on the dance floor. I can still feel the electricity of his forehead against mine and hear the tenderness in his voice. Part of me wants to pinch myself, just to confirm it has all been real.

As I lie in bed, my heart flutters with a mix of excitement and nerves about what the future holds. Will Javier and I see each other again soon? What will happen when I see Amy? Will she still be my friend, or will she give me the cold shoulder? These questions swirl in my mind, making it hard to settle down. What does all of this mean for my time here in Ecuador?

I try to quiet my racing thoughts, knowing I need at least a little sleep before facing the day ahead. But it's hard to calm down when I feel like I'm floating on air. Eventually, with Javier's scent still lingering on my skin, I drift off into a contented sleep, dreaming of our next encounter and the possibilities it holds.

May 29, 1993
MANABÍ

The shrill beeping of the alarm clock pierces through my dreams, jolting me awake. In one smooth motion, I spring out of bed, my feet hitting the floor with an unexpected burst of energy. Despite the sleepless night, I feel alive, electrified by the memories of dancing with Javier.

Señor Rodriguez is taking our cohort to the beach, a place called Manabí. I know my adrenaline and the lack of sleep will eventually catch up with me, but the promise of sun-soaked days ahead seems like the perfect opportunity to rest and bask in the afterglow of last night's magic.

With giddy urgency, I quickly shower and pack my carry-on bag with essentials for the overnight trip. As I head downstairs for breakfast, I find Ramona already seated at the table. Curious but careful not to pry, she asks if I had a good time last night.

I can't help but grin; warmth floods my cheeks as I reply, "It was great." My voice rises slightly in pitch, betraying my excitement. The sparkle in my eyes and my bright expression reveal just how captivated I am by Javier.

A wave of relief washes over me when Ramona doesn't mention the late hour of my return or the fact that I woke her up with my clumsy attempts to sneak in, narrowly avoiding the guard dog. Instead, she simply smiles, and in that moment, I feel a sense of comfort and acceptance. The thrill of the evening still lingers in my heart, and I'm grateful for this incredible experience.

Ramona places a brown paper bag on the edge of the table, her expression warm and thoughtful. She tells me she instructed Nilda to pack it for me—a delicious sandwich made with mortadella, a savory pork lunch meat similar to bologna, paired with cheese. Inside, I also find a ripe banana and a bottle of water, all prepared with care in case I get hungry during the long ride ahead.

Her kindness wraps around me like a comforting hug, and I can't help but feel grateful for her thoughtfulness.

As she drops me off at the university entrance, she waves goodbye and tells me to have a good time. She reminds me she'll be picking me up the following night. Fellow classmates arrive at our meeting place by bus or cab.

Each person climbs into the campus passenger van and places their luggage in the back seat. One by one, we choose our preferred seats and wave for the next person to board. Kate and Amy settle together, with Kate cheerfully calling out, "I got the window!" I pick the seat directly in front of them and happily oblige Sharon's request to sit together. Derek and Julia share a seat on the opposite side of the van, while the seat in front of them is reserved for a cooler filled with lunches, drinks, and other treats for the long ride ahead. Rashad climbs into the passenger seat beside Señor Rodriguez.

Once everyone is settled, Señor Rodriguez turns to us with a grin and exclaims, "Hold on tight!" He merges into the busy flow of traffic, flooring it to avoid the impatient honking from behind. I brace myself, already knowing that not preparing for the sudden jolt could lead to whiplash.

"Tell me about your dates," Sharon prompts, her eyes sparkling with curiosity as she leans in, eager to hear every detail about our big night out.

With Sharon and me turned around in our seats, the conversation flows effortlessly, filled with laughter and animated chatter about meeting up with Javier and his friends, the vibrant music that filled the air, and the sheer joy of learning to dance together.

Amy's eyes sparkle as she gushes about dancing with Mario, her words tumbling out in an excited rush. Sharon's eyebrows raise slightly in surprise, knowing Amy's previous crush on Javier. A wave of relief washes over me as Sharon doesn't question it further.

Though Amy seems to have moved past any hurt feelings over Javier choosing me, I tread carefully, not wanting to risk upsetting her. Our friendship means too much to me to jeopardize it with insensitivity. I focus on listening, offering encouraging smiles and nods.

Meanwhile, Kate's lips curl into a subtle, knowing smile each time her name comes up in the conversation. There's a mischievous glint in her eye that hints at more than she's letting on.

While it's unclear how far she and Alejandro actually explored their attraction, playful, suggestive remarks pepper their story. The innuendos are hard to miss, leaving us all wondering just how steamy their night really was.

I spend the weekend indulging in rest and relaxation. Floating weightlessly in the calm waters of the ocean, I replay our date in my mind—his smoldering eyes staring into my soul and the scent of sandalwood that clung to his skin. A smile tugs at the corners of my lips as I remember the tingles that raced up my spine when his hand found the small of my back, pulling me closer as we swayed to the rhythm of the music.

When he kissed me on the forehead, he implied there would be a next time. But when exactly will that "next time" be?

May 31, 1993
Taken by Surprise

As I stand on the sidewalk, the oppressive heat and humidity cling to me, heightening the mix of anticipation and anxiety swirling in my chest as I try to hail a furgoneta ride home after class. Suddenly, I catch a glimpse of a familiar face—Javier. He's laughing, surrounded by a group of guys, his carefree demeanor a stark contrast to the knot of hope and uncertainty tightening in my stomach.

My heart skips a beat, a rush of emotions flooding over me. I can't help but wonder why he's here. Is he just passing by, or has he come to see me?

When Javier spots me, his expression shifts, and he quickly excuses himself from the group. I watch, heart pounding, as he strides briskly across the courtyard, his smile growing wider with each step. The sight of his cute, boyish dimples makes my stomach flutter, and I can hardly contain my own smile as he approaches.

When he finally stands before me, he opens his arms wide and pulls me into a gentle embrace that feels both warm and exhilarating. As he places a tender kiss on my cheek, a surge of warmth pulses through me, making my heart race.

He pulls back slightly, a playful glint in his eyes. Without a word, he reaches for the heavy bag of textbooks I'm carrying and effortlessly takes it from me.

With a charming wink, he gestures toward an empty bench nearby.

Nodding in agreement, I follow him to the bench and settle down beside him. A wave of happiness washes over me, mingling with a thrilling sense of anticipation for the moment we're about to share.

Javier is curious about how my weekend went and the places I visited. I tell him I spent it in Manabí.

"Manabí, huh?" He seems to know the coastal province well. His eyes never leave my face as he listens intently while I describe, as best I can in Spanish, the bamboo huts with thatched roofs where we stayed. I continue, sharing how in awe I was of the sandy, pristine beaches with shimmering turquoise waters and the breathtaking flora—palms, hibiscus, orchids, and freesia in vibrant pink, orange, red, and yellow peeking through the greenery.

Javier plucks a delicate flower from a nearby bush, its petals a soft lavender hue. "Tú color favorita (Your favorite color)," he points out.

With gentle care, he tucks the stem behind my ear, his fingers stroking my hair. As he adjusts the petals, his fingers linger for a moment on my cheek. "Muy hermosa (Very beautiful)," he murmurs, his eyes locked with mine. "Como tú (Like you)," he adds, his voice filled with sincerity.

He thinks I'm beautiful. He thinks I'm beautiful. Taken aback by Javier's compliment, warmth floods my cheeks, a soft blush spreading across my face. I'm momentarily lost for words, my eyes darting down to escape his intense gaze. "Gracias," I whisper, my voice barely above a breath.

Sensing my slight discomfort, Javier shifts the conversation. "¿Te gustó bailar (Did you like dancing)?" he asks.

My face lights up at the mention of dancing. "Yes, my friends and I really enjoyed our night out," I tell him. Fidgeting with the hem of my shirt, I admit, with a hint of nervous excitement, that it was actually my first time on a date in a club. The memory of the music and the way I danced with him rushes back, filling me with a mix of joy and vulnerability.

"¿En realidad (Really)? ¿Por qué (Why)?" Javier seems surprised.

I explain the age requirements in the United States for entering a club—patrons must be twenty-one years old; I'm only twenty. Javier, a year older than me, nods in understanding. His eyes widen slightly as he realizes the difference, explaining that in his country, there are no such age restrictions.

As we continue to talk, another interesting coincidence comes up. "You know," he says in Spanish, "not only are we just one year apart, but our birthdays are also just a month apart." *How fascinating that our birthdays are so closely aligned!*

Javier asks what I enjoy doing in my free time. I share that I love to read, attend university, meet new people, and learn to speak Spanish.

His eyes sparkle with delight as he listens. Meeting new people is one of his favorite things too. After a brief pause, he tells me that now that he's met me, he wants to learn English.

A warm flutter fills my chest at the thought that he wants to learn English because of me. Each time he attempts an English phrase, no matter how simple, my heart melts.

Even though Javier only speaks Spanish, we find ways to bridge the language gap. Whenever one of us struggles to express a word, we flip through my well-worn Spanish-English dictionary together. Not every word has a perfect translation, but through patience and a shared desire to understand one another, we piece together meanings.

Like most Ecuadorians I've met, Javier is eager to learn everything he can about the United States. It seems his entire reference point for America revolves around New York City. I've visited Manhattan a few times on bus trips to see a Broadway play, the Christmas Spectacular at Radio City Music Hall, and the iconic Rockefeller Center with its Christmas tree and ice skating during the holiday season. While New York City is technically part of my homeland, I'm merely a tourist there. Ironically, Guayaquil is more like New York City than my hometown.

Javier asks if I live near New York. "Sort of," I reply, explaining that I live in Pennsylvania. He jokes, asking if I'm neighbors with Drácula.

Unfazed by his humor, I clarify that I live far from the city, in the countryside, or 'el campo.' I paint a picture of rolling hills and endless farmland where most residents, including my family, have their own gardens.

I tell him that while many locals provide for themselves, others grow crops to sell for profit. I also share that some of my friends' parents are dairy farmers, while others raise livestock like cows, pigs, chickens, sheep, and goats.

As I speak, I notice Javier's eyes light up with fascination, and I feel a warmth in sharing a piece of my world with him. His curiosity and genuine interest in my life back home make me feel a deeper connection to him and remind me of the beauty in exchanging stories and cultures.

June 14, 1993
BREATHTAKING VIEWS

With each passing day, our evening rendezvous evolve into something more—a captivating journey we both cherish. These moments, filled with discovery, offer new insights into each other and our distinct cultures. Each meeting brings new insights, laughter, and shared experiences, deepening our connection and enriching our understanding as we explore beyond the familiar confines of the university campus.

On this balmy evening, we find ourselves in Las Peñas, a vibrant neighborhood that looks like it leapt straight from a postcard with its vivid, contrasting colors. Javier's eyes sparkle with excitement as he asks if I'd like to climb the staircase to the top for the perfect view. Not wanting to seem lazy, I agree, my heart fluttering with a mix of anticipation and trepidation.

Only a few minutes into our ascent, sweat beads on my forehead, and I'm silently cursing my decision. Several times, I suggest stopping, pretending to be interested in the view while secretly longing for a break.

When we finally reach the summit, my breath catches—not just from exertion, but from the breathtaking panorama before us. The view stretches out like a tapestry of lights and colors, making my heart soar. Standing atop Las Peñas, I see the cultural sites of Santa Ana Hills Chapel and the Lighthouse. In this moment, I realize the climb was more than worth it.

Javier, ever attentive, approaches a street vendor. As the vendor skillfully cuts a coconut in half and places straws in the center, I'm struck by the simple beauty of the moment. Javier hands me mine, his smile as refreshing as the drink itself. The sweet taste of the coconut water floods my senses, and suddenly, I'm transported back to a conversation with Mayra about Ramona, her words echoing in my mind: "faro de luz (beacon of light)."

In this perfect moment, high above the city with Javier by my side, I feel a profound connection—not just to him, but to all the stories and experiences others have shared. The taste of coconut, the twinkling lights below, and the warmth of Javier's presence all blend into a tapestry of emotion, reminding me of the beautiful complexity of life and love in this vibrant, new place.

June 15, 1993
Fascination with Fashion

Hand in hand, we wander through the bustling streets, our eyes dancing over the vibrant window displays. Javier's fascination with fashion is endearing; his eyes light up with childlike wonder at each storefront we pass.

He excitedly rattles off the names of renowned designers—Ralph Lauren, Calvin Klein, Tommy Hilfiger—his enthusiasm infectious. I can't help but smile at his passion, feeling a warmth spread through me as I watch him revel in the beauty around us.

While I don't share Javier's love for fashion trends and designer labels, finding most outfits bizarre and impractical, I can't help but enjoy the pure joy it brings him. His excitement is a beautiful thing to witness, and I find myself falling more in love with his unbridled enthusiasm for life.

When I tell Javier about meeting Miss Ecuador at a university event, his eyes widen with genuine interest. "Really? She's from Guayas?" he asks, barely containing his excitement. I beam with pride, eager to tell him that I learned in class that Guayas is the largest of Ecuador's twenty-four provinces, with Guayaquil as its bustling capital.

Javier's face beams as he adds, "And she grew up near Manabí!" My heart swells with warmth, remembering my own adventures there during one of my first weekends in the country.

His enthusiasm is contagious, and I lean in closer as he shares another fascinating detail, his voice brimming with pride: "Did you know Miss Ecuador's mom held the same title back in 1964?" I'm amazed by how much Javier knows about her, even though he's never met her.

While fashion isn't typically my forte, I find myself swept up in the conversation. Memories of watching beauty pageants back home, especially Miss Universe, flash through my mind. I recall the breathtaking array of ethnic costumes, each telling a story of its country's culture and heritage.

Curiosity piqued, I pause for a moment, silently wondering what Miss Ecuador will wear to represent her country. With Ecuador's rich diversity—from the Andes to the Amazon to the coast—I can only imagine the stunning options she might have.

As I recount my experience, I explain how meeting the beauty queen felt like encountering a celebrity. Magazines often depict her as a glamorous figure, perfectly poised among a sea of contestants in swimsuits, evening gowns, and ethnic dresses. But in that setting, she wasn't fretting over hair, makeup, or modeling in high heels. Instead, she blended in humbly with the crowd. What impressed me most was her warm and cheerful personality, which shone brighter than any crown.

Javier listens intently, his eyes soft with understanding. The connection we share feels profound, as if each new piece of information brings us closer, strengthening our bond even more.

June 16, 1993
ENCHANTED BY HIS ATTENTION

A long the picturesque bay, the air pulses with vibrant rhythms from local musicians, the lively beats of merengue intertwining with the sultry sounds of salsa. As we pause to soak in the music, I catch a glimpse of mischief sparkling in Javier's eyes. He tugs gently on my hand, his playful grin inviting me to join him. "¿Bailamos?" he asks.

A smile spreads across my face, warmth blooming within me. Other couples are dancing, their joy infectious, and I feel a rush of courage. With a simple nod, Javier leads me to a small open space near the musicians, their colorful instruments gleaming in the warm evening light.

His fingers intertwine with mine, a connection that sends tingles through my body. Turning to face me, he places his right hand on my waist, his touch both reassuring and electric.

In the discoteca, we were confined to a small space on the dance floor, but here, the world opens up around us, inviting us to let loose and embrace the rhythm.

With gentle guidance, he steers me through turns and steps I never knew I could make. As I twirl under his arm, an exhilarating sense of freedom and joy washes over me—an experience I've never known before.

The music wraps around us like a warm embrace, and I lose myself in the moment, laughing and spinning, my heart racing in time with the vibrant beat. Each movement feels like a celebration, a dance not just of bodies but of souls intertwining in the magic of the night.

June 17, 1993
FÚTBOL

While strolling through the park, the sight of children playing soccer draws us in. Their tiny cleats kick up small clouds of grass, their laughter and shouts of excitement filling the air as they chase the black-and-white ball up and down the field. The scene stirs something within me, a mix of nostalgia.

"¿Te gusta?" Javier asks, his eyes twinkling with curiosity.

I smile, memories of my own childhood flooding back, and tell him I played soccer as a kid.

Javier's face lights up, his passion evident as he declares, "Fútbol está en mi corazón (Soccer is in my heart)." The sincerity in his voice touches me, and I can see how deeply the sport means to him.

Feeling a bit sheepish, I admit that despite knowing soccer's importance in South America, I've never experienced a professional game firsthand. Javier's eyes widen with surprise.

"Would you like to go to a game?" he asks, his voice filled with excitement and anticipation. My heart skips a beat at the invitation, thrilled at the prospect of sharing this experience with him.

"I'd love to!" I reply eagerly, my enthusiasm matching his. The idea of going anywhere with Javier fills me with joy, but the thought of experiencing his passion for soccer firsthand is especially thrilling.

June 21, 1993
Tickets to Copa America

Javier's excited to share that he managed to get tickets for one of the Copa America semifinal games—Colombia vs. Argentina. His eyes sparkle with delight, and I can't help but be swept up in his enthusiasm. The magnitude of the event—a tournament on par with the World Cup—starts to sink in, and a mix of excitement and nervous anticipation bubbles up inside me.

As I look at Javier's beaming face, I realize this isn't just about watching a game. It's about sharing a piece of his heart, his culture, and his passion. The prospect of experiencing this with him fills me with a warmth that spreads from my chest to the tips of my fingers, a feeling of connection and anticipation for the unforgettable experience that awaits us.

June 23, 1993
Driven by Passion

The stadium pulses with energy as I find myself immersed in the colors of the Ecuadorian flag—a vibrant sea of yellow, blue, and red. Even though the semifinal match is a fierce showdown between Colombia and Argentina, the air is thick with an overwhelming allegiance to Argentina, alive with spirited chants echoing: "Ar-gen-tina, Ar-gen-tina!"

My attention is irresistibly drawn to Javier, whose eyes are glued to the field, each skillful play igniting gasps of anticipation with every near miss. As the tension builds, a collective heartbeat echoes through the stands, uniting us in shared hope and excitement, fueling the passion in the air.

Then, in a moment that feels suspended in time, the ball strikes the back of the net. An explosion of cheers erupts from the crowd. Argentina has scored! Strangers become instant friends, embracing one another and swirling in a passionate dance of celebration.

Caught up in the excitement, I leap to my feet, adrenaline coursing through me as I cheer alongside the thrumming crowd.

As the match continues to unfold, the atmosphere shifts. Alcohol flows freely, and the intoxication among fans leads to chaotic frenzy. Yelling and booing fill the air with every steal and failed attempt at a goal. Out of the corner of my eye, I can't believe what I'm seeing. Some of the inebriated spectators are urinating in plastic bags.

When the final whistle blows, signaling a tie between the two teams, those same bags are hurled onto the field. I stare in disbelief, appalled by the scene unfolding before me.

Eager to escape the madness that has overtaken the stadium, Javier grabs my hand, urgency in his grip as we exit the stands and hurry away from the chaos.

Once we're safely inside his car, Javier turns to me with an eager smile, asking how I enjoyed the game. I respond enthusiastically, expressing my appreciation for the sport and its popularity in his country. However, beneath my polite exterior, I'm still reeling from the shocking scenes I witnessed.

The memory of grown men brazenly urinating into bags and then hurling them onto the field is an image I can't seem to shake. I struggle to reconcile this behavior with the excitement and passion I felt during the match. What surprises me even more is Javier's nonchalant attitude. While I expected him to share my discomfort, he seems unfazed, as if this were perfectly normal. His casual acceptance of such a bizarre and unsettling act leaves me feeling bewildered and out of place.

As we merge with traffic and drive away from the stadium, I'm left grappling with this cultural disconnect, trying to make sense of an experience that was both thrilling and deeply unsettling.

Outside the city limits, Javier unexpectedly steers the car off the main road, pulling into a secluded area.

The engine falls silent, and I find myself in unfamiliar surroundings, though I suspect we're not far from my home.

With careful intention, Javier rolls down his window, then leans across the gearshift to lower mine, his closeness sending a delightful shiver down my spine. As he brushes his cheek against mine, his voice drops to a hushed whisper, "Solo tú y yo (Only you and I)."

His words send my heart racing, the thrill of being alone with him mingling with a growing sense of unease. We're isolated, surrounded by emptiness, with no signs of life or civilization in sight, and his intentions remain a mystery.

A playful, mischievous smile dances on Javier's lips as he draws me closer, our eyes locking in a gaze so intense it feels like he can see into my very soul. Leaning forward, his lips capture mine in a swift, tender kiss.

"Te quiero," he whispers, the words hanging in the air between us, heavy with meaning.

My pulse races, a whirlwind of butterflies swirling in my stomach. I glance down, unconsciously wetting my lips as I struggle to catch my breath. Gathering my courage, I look up and breathe my response, "Te quiero también." The words carry the unmistakable longing and affection I feel.

Heat and humidity quickly invade the cool space, the air crackling with anticipation, every nerve in my body alive and tingling with desire. But just as our lips are about to meet again, the harsh glare of approaching headlights cuts through the darkness, shattering our intimate bubble. The spell of our moonlit rendezvous breaks, leaving us both breathless and yearning, the moment of passion interrupted but far from forgotten.

Javier hastily restarts the car and drives directly to the address of my host family. As I exit the car and grab my bag from the backseat, he extends his hand to touch my arm. Gazing into each other's eyes once more, he mouths the words, "Hasta mañana."

"Hasta mañana," I whisper back, the promise of tomorrow lingering in the air.

June 28, 1993
FOOD POISONING

O n Monday morning, I wake up feeling light-headed and nauseous, a heavy dread settling in my stomach. The temptation to stay in bed all day is strong, but the thought of missing a chance to see Javier tugs at my heart. I haven't seen him since last Wednesday, and each day apart feels like an eternity. Weekends are reserved for family time or sightseeing with my American friends, so I only get to see him during the week, after my evening class.

As the day wears on, my classmates notice my discomfort. During siesta, Kate looks at me with concern. "Are you sure you're okay?" she asks. Sharon suggests I go home, but I stubbornly refuse, insisting I'll be fine. I can't bear the thought of missing Javier.

At lunch, I sit listlessly in the café, my head resting in my hand as I sip ginger ale through a straw. The air conditioning at Policentro feels particularly cold, yet beads of sweat form on my forehead, and my skin is clammy.

By the time my evening class begins, my face is flushed, and I'm shivering despite the heat radiating from my body. I must have a fever. Throughout the day, I've made multiple sprints to the bathroom, praying each time that I'd make it in time.

Señor Gomez enters the classroom, his eyes immediately sensing something is wrong. Derek pulls him aside, explaining that I've been unwell all day but refuse to go home.

With quiet concern, Señor Gomez steps out of the room. When he returns, he gently places his hand on my shoulder and tells me that Señor Rodriguez is coming to take me to the hospital. Derek leans over, promising to let Javier know I'm not standing him up.

The ride to the hospital is uncomfortable, pain twisting my insides as I pray to make it there before another urgent bathroom trip. At the hospital, my vital signs reveal a low-grade fever, and blood work shows severe dehydration. The medical team starts an IV to replenish my fluids and administers medication for the pain. The diagnosis is bacterial gastroenteritis—food poisoning.

Over the weekend, my family and I celebrated Father's Day at a local restaurant. I had tried crab ceviche, thinking it would be as delicious as the shrimp ceviche I'd loved. Now, it's presumed the crab wasn't cooked before being marinated. Despite others having the same dish, I fell ill—my body unaccustomed to the local waters.

As I lie in the hospital bed, the events of the day blur together. My heart aches with the longing to see Javier, and the fear of missing out on our time together weighs heavily on me. Yet, amid the discomfort, there's a flicker of hope that this will pass, and soon I'll be back on my feet, ready to embrace the moments that await.

Ramona rushes into the room, her face etched with serious concern. Despite having already spoken with Señor Rodriguez on the phone about my prognosis, she still has questions for the doctor. The nurse removes the IV, and the recommended medications are thoroughly reviewed: Ciproflaxin, to be taken twice a day for the next five days, and a variation of Pepto-Bismol for pain and diarrhea as needed. The hospital pharmacy has already filled the prescriptions.

As Ramona pulls up in front of our home, Mayra stands by the gate, anxiously waiting to welcome me back. She lifts my heavy bag of textbooks from the back of the van and carries it upstairs for me.

I thank Mayra for carrying my books. Though my hands are empty, I struggle with the simple task of climbing the stairs. Out of breath and needing to take several breaks, the climb feels particularly steep and never-ending. Once I reach my bedroom, all I want to do is lie down. After changing into a sleeveless nightgown, I collapse onto the bed.

Over the next few hours, I sleep soundly in my full-size bed. Mayra, curled up at the bottom, watches over my recovery.

When I wake up in the early hours of the morning, Mayra is right by my side, ready to spring into action. I sit on the side of the bed, doubled over in excruciating pain. The loud, gurgling noises from my stomach signal that I need to use the bathroom. I hesitate, unsure if I can make it there without an accident.

Mayra sees me clutching my midsection, drenched in sweat. In a flash, she's by my side, steadying me as I find my footing and slowly walk across the room.

Unfortunately, despite the short distance to the bathroom, I don't make it in time. Watery, loose stools run down my leg, leaving puddles along the way. Behind the shower curtain, I hand Mayra my soiled nightgown and underwear. A fresh pair of pajamas and undergarments await me after a quick, cold shower.

Over the next thirty-six hours, I experience at least half a dozen similar episodes. With only one nightgown and a pair of pajamas, I'm now just in a cotton top and panties. Thankfully, I have a two-week supply of underwear.

Bottled water, Gatorade, and chicken broth are brought to my bedside, but I can't seem to keep anything down. Mayra holds my hair back as I vomit, rubs my back, and pats my forehead and face with cold compresses.

Sitting on the tiled floor with my head hanging over the toilet becomes my preferred position, though more often than not, the unannounced regurgitation soils my bedding, which then needs changing.

Ramona insists I can't go to school until I can eat solid food. As I begin regaining my strength, I'm encouraged to venture downstairs and eat at the dining room table. Finally graduating to solid food, I'm excited to see what's been prepared for me. I've built up quite an appetite.

Sadly, my appetite vanishes when I see what's in the bowl—broth with beef, a piece of corn on the cob, potatoes, green plantains, fresh oregano, and yucca. I absolutely hate yucca; to me, it's more like 'yucko.'

Ramona notices my disappointment and places a comforting hand on my shoulder, asking what's wrong. Not wanting to hurt anyone's feelings but knowing I can't endure the texture without getting sick again, I express my distaste for yucca.

Ramona is dumbfounded when I admit to disliking the hearty root. Whenever a meal included yucca, I'd eat it first. Unbeknownst to her, my family, particularly my father, was very strict about meals. Growing up, I was forced to sample everything on my plate and eat every morsel before leaving the table. I learned to eat what I disliked first so that the last taste in my mouth was something I enjoyed.

By scarfing down the yucca first, my Ecuadorian family assumed it was a favorite. In fact, Nilda tried to include yucca with every meal. Once the truth is revealed, we laugh about the misunderstanding as the yucca is removed from the bowl.

I ask if I can attend my evening class, secretly hoping to see Javier.

"Muy bien, mi hija," Ramona responds.

Ramona offers to drive me to school and drops me off in front of the university. With class about to start, I have no time to waste.

Everyone is relieved to see me feeling better. "We were really worried about you," Amy says.

After class, I head to the courtyard, waiting for almost half an hour before accepting that Javier isn't coming.

July 8, 1993
GALÁPAGOS ISLANDS

During lunch, Sharon excitedly proposes a trip to the Galápagos Islands—a three-day, two-night excursion for seven hundred dollars per person, covering airfare, hotel accommodations, and meals. Seeking companionship, she invites others from our group. I'm captivated by the glossy brochures she picked up from a downtown travel agency and consider this rare opportunity, even though my knowledge of the islands is limited.

That evening, I discuss the potential trip with Javier. The thought of being apart for two nights is unsettling, especially with the end of my studies approaching and our impending separation looming over us. Yet, Javier encourages me to go. He's never been to the Galápagos Islands and doesn't want me to miss out on this unique adventure.

Seeking further guidance, I reach out to my parents. They, too, enthusiastically support my decision to embark on this once-in-a-lifetime journey.

During our two-hour flight from Guayaquil to the Galápagos Islands, Sharon and I find out that the young man sharing our row is from Greece. While Sharon and I will stay on Santa Cruz Island and travel to and from this hub for our excursions each day, Nikolas will board a cruise ship and tour the islands through various ports of call.

After landing on Baltra Island, we're shuttled to a boat for a ten-minute ferry ride across the Itabaca Channel. Upon reaching the dock on Santa Cruz, we board an overcrowded bus bound for Puerto Ayora, the island's main town. Several older patrons offer their seats to Sharon and me, but we politely decline. Instead, we stand in the aisle with others, gripping the tops of nearby seats for balance while straddling our carry-on bags.

Despite the discomfort from constant swaying for the next forty-five minutes, my standing position offers an unparalleled view of the island's remarkable fauna. My eyes widen in amazement as I spot giant tortoises roaming freely across the terrain, their massive shells and lumbering gait far larger than I had imagined.

After settling into our room, Sharon and I head out to explore the island. Carlo, our tour guide, leads us to a spot where we can safely observe and photograph the giant tortoises. We're not allowed to touch them, but we can kneel nearby for photos. As we take turns posing, one of the gentle giants extends its neck, as if posing for the camera.

Another remarkable resident we encounter on our first day is the blue-footed booby. I giggle at the peculiar name. Carlo explains that "booby" comes from the Spanish word "bobo," meaning "stupid." Like the tortoises, these clumsy birds with webbed blue feet are fearless around humans.

As we approach to take photos, I notice white material on the rocks and ground surrounding the birds.

Curious, I whisper to Sharon, wondering if it's bird droppings. Carlo, overhearing, laughs and apologizes for his oversight. He tells us the white substance is actually chalk, used to mark the boundaries that visitors must respect while exploring the area.

I spot two small eggs under one of the birds and a fluffy white puff under another. At first, I think the bird has molted and shed some old feathers. However, as I detect movement, I realize the fluff is actually a baby booby snuggled under its mother's protective feet.

A whistling noise catches my attention. One of the birds flaps its wings, pointing its beak and tail in the air, almost as if showing off its feet. Carlo explains that this is exactly what the bird is doing. At that moment, we're witnessing the mating dance of the male blue-footed booby. Coincidentally, the finer the feet, the more appealing the mate.

As I quietly continue to watch, this perfect gentleman approaches the lady he's trying to court and offers her a stick from his mouth. "Oh my, it's as if he's proposing," I say.

"Exactly," Carlo replies. He adds that once the male attracts a female, it's common for them to remain a couple for life.

I can't help but wonder, "Will Javier and I be a couple for life?"

Carlo accompanies Sharon and me back to our hotel, his face warm with a genuine smile as we thank him and tip him for his wonderful guidance. Bowing slightly, he says, "Mi placer (My pleasure)." Pointing back in the direction from which we came, he assures us he'll see us tomorrow at six o'clock in the morning.

Filled with a mix of anxious excitement and the realization that we need to rise early, I reluctantly agree to retreat to the room I'm sharing with Sharon. I can't remember the last time I went to bed so early. Normally, at eight o'clock in the evening, I'd still be with Javier, savoring every moment together.

As I glance out the window, I watch the island's nightlife begin to stir, the lively music gradually drowning out the sound of Sharon's snores. Even though not even a freight train could wake her from her deep sleep, I still tiptoe around the room, careful not to disturb her. I write a few postcards, telling friends and family that I miss home; however, this couldn't be further from the truth. The thought of leaving Javier, my friends, and family here fills me with dread.

Surprisingly, as soon as I climb into my twin bed, exhaustion overtakes me, and I drift off to sleep, the anticipation of tomorrow's adventures mingling with the bittersweet awareness of my limited time left in this beautiful place.

I'm already wide awake when the alarm clock beeps at five o'clock in the morning. Excitement bubbles within me as I step into my bathing suit, feeling refreshed and ready for a day filled with new discoveries. I pull on blue shorts and a cotton floral shirt over my one-piece, but as I step outside, I'm surprised by a little nip in the air, prompting me to grab the lightweight purple jacket I packed.

Knowing that sightseers are encouraged to fuel up on a hearty breakfast, Sharon and I dutifully follow the advice. In the cozy hospitality nook of our modest bed and breakfast, we help ourselves to a complimentary breakfast, the aroma of fresh coffee and pastries filling the air.

As I step onto the wood-framed dock, Carlo rushes over to us, his face lighting up with joy. "¡Buenos días! ¿Cómo has dormido (Good morning. How did you sleep)?" he exclaims, his arms open wide.

In unison, Sharon and I respond, "We slept well," our voices filled with the thrill of the day ahead.

"¡Chévere!" he beams.

Once all fifteen passengers are aboard the motor-powered boat, Carlo introduces us to his crew, all of whom will be accompanying us to North Seymour Island. One by one, each passenger introduces themselves to the group—David and Diana, honeymooners from Spain; Elena, a native of Loja, with her friend Ibrahim visiting from Saudi Arabia; Lupe from Portovelo, accompanied by her sister, husband, and three adorable nieces from Guatemala; Lars, a freelance photographer from Holland; and Ares and Ben, from Finland, backpacking through South America. Sharon and I are the only travelers from the United States, and I feel a sense of camaraderie forming among us.

In his charming, broken English, Carlo explains that park guidelines prevent docking on uninhabited islands, so we'll anchor a short distance from shore and shuttle four to five passengers at a time using a smaller watercraft called a dinghy. To protect the precious wildlife, the government also limits the number of boats allowed to cruise around the islands. While we sail together today, future excursions might be with other groups.

As we navigate the crystal blue waters of the Pacific Ocean, I spot dolphins frolicking in the distance, their playful leaps filling me with joy. As the landmasses come into focus, I excitedly point out, "Look at the seals!"

My observation is quickly corrected—what I thought were seals are actually sea lions. In the water, both marine mammals look similar, but sea lions can walk on land using their large flippers, while seals have much smaller flippers and must wriggle on their bellies.

A gust of wind sweeps a colorful pink and coral cap off one little girl's head, sending it tumbling into the water. Though Lydia will likely never see her cap again, it's delightful to watch the playful pups tossing it back and forth, their instinctive playfulness shining through. The crowd claps as they put on an impromptu show, their antics a reminder of the joy found in nature.

Once we reach the shoreline, I grasp Berto's extended hand, trying to find my balance on land. The ground is covered in black volcanic rock and cacti, a stark contrast to the tropical paradise I had imagined. Thankful for my sneakers, I quickly understand why hiking boots and water shoes were recommended.

The uneven black rock, with its jagged edges, makes walking a challenge. Carefully placing one foot in front of the other, my legs tire from the effort to stabilize myself. I can't help but think sea lions have an easier time navigating this terrain than I do. With this realization, I decide not to venture too far.

Large rocks along the water's edge are claimed by iguanas, their short, blunt snouts and small, razor-like teeth giving them a monstrous appearance. Exclusively found on the Galápagos Islands, I learn that the marine iguana eats algae and is the only lizard in the world capable of living at sea. They sit completely still, posing perfectly as I snap several pictures.

Bright red shellfish, known as the Sally Lightfoot crab, lounge in the sun on the black lava rocks. While the marine iguanas seem unfazed by our presence, the crabs scurry between the rocks at the slightest hint of movement, evading our attempts to capture their image. Normally, I wouldn't mind their avoidance, as I'm not particularly fond of these crustaceans, but I still want to document the moment. Capturing a picture of the crabs feels like a game of hide-and-seek.

While I'm focused on taking photographs, a sea lion barks loudly nearby, almost as if to say, "Don't forget me!" It's fascinating to see them slide right up to our group, curious and unafraid.

"¿Cuánto tiempo te quedas en la isla (How long are you staying on the island)?" asks Rico as Sharon and I step off the boat.

Sharon explains that it's a two-night trip; we arrived yesterday, so tonight is our last night.

Pointing to a nightclub with outdoor seating on a huge deck, Rico suggests we join the crew for drinks and dancing. Initially apprehensive, I can't hide the disappointment on my face, and Sharon, noticing, concedes and agrees. After all, with the festivities not starting until eleven o'clock, she has time to catch a quick siesta.

As I step out of my bathing suit and take a quick shower, I glance at my skin and realize I've gotten sunburned. My lines are nothing compared to Sharon's, though. She's fire engine red and hot to the touch; it will be a miracle if her skin doesn't peel and blister. Before lying down for a nap, we both apply aloe, helping each other with the harder-to-reach spots.

Four hours later, I wake up feeling refreshed and ready to explore the nightlife, while Sharon, unfortunately, is in a lot of discomfort with a slight headache—likely from too much sun exposure, dehydration, or the fact that we haven't eaten in hours.

Dressed in the same shorts and shirts we wore earlier, we head to the dining area for a light dinner. Our waiter takes one look at Sharon and asks, "¿Puedo (May I)?"

With a nod of permission, he gently places his hand on her arm, inquiring if it hurts. The tenderness of his touch reveals the pain she's in.

When he returns to the table, he brings a few packets of aspirin and advises her to take them for inflammation and drink lots of water. He also hands her a plastic container with a clear substance inside. Cautiously lifting the lid, Sharon grimaces at the strong, pungent scent. I lean in to take a whiff. Vinegar?

"¡Whoa!" I exclaim.

"It will help with the pain," he reassures us.

Sharon thanks the generous stranger for the aspirin and vinegar, offering to pay him, but he graciously declines. Instead, she leaves a crispy twenty-dollar bill as a tip.

The aspirin and vinegar seem to provide some relief, but now Sharon walks around smelling like something rotten. She doesn't find it amusing, so I try not to laugh too much, fearing it might mean she won't go dancing after all.

The outdoor party is already in full swing by the time Sharon and I arrive. Its vibrant music pulses through the air, so loud and lively that it feels as if the whole island has come alive to celebrate. The vibrations resonate within me, and for a moment, I can almost believe the ground is shaking beneath my feet.

Across the room, a group of girls from the hotel spot us and wave frantically, calling out, "¡Ven a bailar (Come dance)!" Their enthusiasm is infectious, and I eagerly accept the invitation to join them, while Sharon opts to sit back and watch.

The atmosphere is electric, filled with travelers from all corners of the globe. Instead of the traditional Spanish rhythms of merengue and salsa, the air is alive with dance music—house, electro, and reggae beats dominate the scene. When "Mr. Vain" by the German group Culture Beat plays, I instantly recognize the familiar techno beat, a nostalgic reminder of home.

Seated across the room at the bar is Rico, one of the guides from my tour. He stands tall and muscular, with dark suntanned skin, a testament to long days spent working on the water. His short hair is styled with long bangs slicked back, highlighting his chiseled features— an elongated face with high cheekbones and a defined chin that makes him look like a perfectly sculpted statue. The girls I'm dancing with whisper that he's "hot," and

I can't help but agree; he's undeniably attractive, and he knows it.

Most people on the dance floor have drinks in their hands, but I decline the offers of beer and exotic cocktails. "Agua, por favor," I say.

Later in the evening, a friend encourages me to try some of her sangría, a red punch filled with fruit. I take a sip, completely unaware that it's an alcoholic beverage. The sweet taste is delightful, and I find myself wanting more.

Unbeknownst to me, Rico has been watching me all day. As he approaches me on the dance floor, the crowd erupts in giddy cheers, and I feel a rush of excitement. "Sí, tendré otra sangría (Sure, I'll have another sangría)," I say, the words rolling off my tongue far too easily by the time Sharon expresses her desire to leave.

I lose track of how many sangrías I've had. I'm oblivious to Sharon's discomfort as she sits alone, not wanting to be a party pooper. As long as I'm okay with walking back to the hotel with the other girls, she decides to call it a night.

As the alcohol begins to take effect, so do Rico's hands. Lost in the music, my thoughts drift back to the songs I danced to with Javier on our first date, and I forget who I'm dancing with.

At the end of the night, I join the group of girls as we walk back together. Rico wraps his arm around my neck, pulling me close, and it feels as if everyone watching us has already pegged us as a couple. No one seems surprised when he leads me into a dark, unlit alleyway, away from the crowd.

Once we're alone, he backs me into a corner, pressing his body against mine as he kisses my neck. The words "Te quiero" slip from his lips, whispered in my ear.

In that moment, I snap out of my trance. Less than a month ago, Javier whispered those same words to me, but his declaration had been filled with love and sincerity. In stark contrast, Rico's intentions feel predatory, and I realize he's trying to seduce me for his own gratification.

Pushing Rico away, I firmly state, "Tengo un novio en Guayaquil (I have a boyfriend in Guayaquil)."

He immediately steps back, his arms raised in a gesture of truce. Thankfully, he doesn't seem too put off by my rejection.

It's late, and I'm still feeling the effects of the alcohol. Most importantly, my friends have left, and I still need him to guide me back to the hotel.

As soon as I fall asleep, the alarm clock jolts me awake.

"How was your night? I didn't even hear you come in," Sharon asks, her voice groggy.

"It was fun," I reply, but I can't shake the unease that lingers in my chest.

An upset stomach and pounding headache greet me. Knowing the bathroom might be an issue, I stick to a simple breakfast of just a banana and a plain piece of toast. I take two aspirins from the packets the waiter offered Sharon yesterday, hoping it will quell what I assume is a hangover—something I've never experienced before.

Today, instead of returning to Santa Cruz at the end of the excursion, we fly back to Guayaquil. As we board the dock with our carry-ons, I can feel the stares of others. Just my luck—the girls from last night are on the same boat tour. I can only imagine the assumptions they've made about what happened when I was left alone with Rico.

Despite the tension that hangs between Rico and me, he approaches with a newfound sincerity, apologizing for misreading my body language. I know I wasn't entirely innocent in the situation, so I offer my apology. He accepts it graciously and begins assisting guests with boarding the boat.

Lying in my bed, a whirlwind of 'what ifs' swirls through my mind—What if I hadn't accepted that first sangría? What if I was at fault for leading Rico on? What if he hadn't taken no for an answer? What if Javier ever found out?

What happened during my trip to the Galápagos Islands is not something I ever need to share. I'm grateful to have emerged unscathed—at least physically. It's a lesson learned, one that will linger in my thoughts long after I return home.

July 12, 1993
A NIGHT OF INTIMACY

My time studying abroad has quickly come to a bittersweet end. As I prepare to leave, a wave of emotions washes over me. Most of my cohort has already returned to the United States, and soon a new group of students will fill the spaces we leave behind.

Reflecting on my journey, I feel overwhelmed with gratitude for the friendships I've forged and the incredible experiences I've had. Immersing myself in the vibrant culture and visiting some of the most awe-inspiring places on Earth has been transformative. No textbook could ever capture the authenticity of what I've lived here.

Ecuador, often labeled a third-world country due to its high poverty rates, offered me a unique perspective. Living with a wealthy family, I was sheltered from many hardships, yet I witnessed the resilience and generosity of the people. Despite lacking monetary wealth, their spirit of community and kindness is something I will deeply miss.

Amid the hustle and bustle of city life, people always found time to connect, engage sincerely, and share their stories. The warmth and openness often led to conversations that made me feel truly seen and heard.

The laid-back lifestyle, with its disregard for strict schedules, was both endearing and challenging. While

I appreciate the slower pace and the emphasis on living in the moment, my punctual nature sometimes clashed with the cultural norm of tardiness. Despite my efforts, I couldn't quite embrace this aspect of the culture, but it taught me patience and adaptability.

Saying goodbye to my professors and friends from the university is far more emotional than I anticipated. We exchange addresses, pose for pictures, and promise to keep in touch. Among my group is Javier, who manages to sneak into two of the snapshots. In one, he creatively positions himself between Amy and me—a fitting reminder of how we met, thanks to Amy's initial crush on him. The second picture, just Javier and me, captures the essence of young love. We're beaming, standing close, oblivious to the world around us.

From the moment our eyes met across a crowded room, there was an undeniable connection. Each moment spent together deepened my feelings, and soon he consumed my thoughts. As I prepare to leave, I've made plans to spend my last night in this heartwarming country with him. The thought of saying goodbye is daunting, yet I'm filled with hope and gratitude for the time we've shared.

With trembling hands, I bid a final farewell to my friends, my heart heavy with the bittersweet weight of goodbyes. As their voices fade into the background, I turn to find Javier waiting for me, his eyes sparkling with a mix of excitement and tenderness. Unable to contain his eagerness any longer, he gently takes my hand, a mischievous glint dancing in his gaze.

The sadness of parting from my friends begins to melt away, replaced by a thrilling anticipation of what's to come. I willingly let Javier lead me away from the group, my pulse quickening with each step.

As we wander off alone together, the bustling world around us seems to fade away, leaving just the two of us in our own private universe. The night stretches before us, full of promise and possibility, and I can't help but feel that this goodbye is also the beginning of something beautiful and profound.

As we approach his gray Suzuki Forsa parked nearby, my heart begins to race. Each step feels charged with anticipation, and I can hardly breathe as he opens the passenger door for me. Settling into the seat, a flutter of butterflies erupts in my stomach, a mix of thrill and melancholy.

Alone at last, Javier places his hand on my arm, gently nudging me to face him. His thumb caresses my cheekbone, a tender gesture that sends my heart racing. When our lips finally meet, I open my mouth, allowing his tongue to softly intertwine with mine, deepening our connection in a moment of shared intimacy that feels both exhilarating and terrifying.

Just a short distance from the university, Javier parallel parks along the street and exclaims, "¡Estamos aquí! My home." The warmth in his voice makes my heart swell, but the reality of leaving him soon looms over me like a dark cloud.

Javier takes my hand, his touch sending a shiver of anticipation through me as he leads me to the front door of his place. He asks me to wait, so I stand in the doorway, one foot inside, my heart racing as I discreetly survey his simple studio apartment.

As my eyes sweep to the left, I'm drawn to a cozy kitchenette—a compact refrigerator and a small gas stove nestled against the back wall, a petite sink, and two stools beneath a counter. A stack of glossy fashion magazines catches my eye, perched on a nearby metal stand, confirming Javier's passions and refined tastes. My heart flutters with excitement, feeling a deeper connection to him through these small glimpses into his world.

Before I can absorb more of my surroundings, Javier returns, his presence electrifying the air around us. He gently takes my hands in his, the warmth of his touch sending shivers down my spine. As he pulls me forward, I hear the soft click of the door locking behind us, the sound sealing us in our own intimate universe, making my pulse quicken with anticipation.

A few steps in, my breath catches as my gaze falls upon Javier's bed, adorned with a striking black-and-white striped comforter. My heart races as I take in the full-length mirror leaning against the wall, framed by pictures of chiseled male models showcasing the latest fashion trends. Each image seems to pulse with the same allure and charisma that drew me to Javier.

The room thrums with his essence, every carefully chosen element a vibrant reflection of his magnetic personality. I'm engulfed by a dizzying whirlwind of emotions—nervousness and exhilaration intertwining, leaving me breathless. The intimacy of the moment washes over me, and I'm acutely aware of the depth of my feelings for him, threatening to overwhelm me completely.

As my eyes adjust to the soft lighting, I'm struck speechless by the effort Javier has made to make our last night together unforgettable. A vanilla-scented candle flickers beside the bed, its warm, inviting glow dancing across the walls, casting intimate shadows. Gentle instrumental music fills the air, wrapping around us like a tender embrace.

Words seem to evaporate on my tongue, rendered unnecessary by the intensity of the moment. The sparkle in Javier's eyes speaks volumes, reflecting a depth of emotion that makes my heart soar and my knees weak. In this perfect, passion-filled cocoon, I feel more cherished and desired than ever before.

Javier pulls me closer, our fingers intertwining as we hold each other tight. I rest my head on his shoulder, feeling the steady rhythm of his heart against my chest. "Thump thump, thump thump"—it echoes my own racing pulse, our hearts beating in perfect synchronicity.

Our breath quickens as our hips sway to the music, our bodies moving as one fluid entity. "Si el tiempo se detuviera (If only time stood still)," Javier whispers, a bittersweet reminder of our fleeting time together.

As I inhale deeply, the intoxicating aroma of Obsession for Men envelops me. The rich, seductive hints of sandalwood caress my senses, igniting a fire deep within. Yet, despite its name, there's nothing controlling about our connection. In our brief time together, I've never felt more cherished and secure.

In this moment, wrapped in his arms, I truly feel as though time has stood still, allowing us to savor every precious second of our bond.

Being with Javier has awakened a newfound confidence in me—one I've never experienced before. His presence empowers me, making me feel invincible and genuinely alive. The fragrance lingers on my skin, a constant reminder of the safety and security I feel in his embrace.

With every breath, I'm wrapped in a cocoon of warmth and love, mirroring the tenderness of our relationship. The scent has become more than just a cologne; it's a symbol of the profound connection we share, a testament to the way Javier makes me feel—desired, respected, and completely free to be myself.

I feel the warmth of his lips on my earlobe, his gentle touch sending shivers down my spine as he begins tickling my torso. As he leans in, his gaze steady and intense, I tilt my head, my breath catching as his lips graze mine.

His tongue slips into my mouth, intensifying my desire. I run my hands through his hair, my eyes closing as I lose myself in the passionate moment, savoring every sensation and committing it to memory.

The freedom of having no curfew is comforting, allowing the evening to unfold at its own unhurried pace. The relief of not having to constantly look over our shoulders is intoxicating, and we revel in the luxury of taking our time. Every sense is heightened as we focus on each sight, sound, smell, taste, and movement.

Our lips remain locked in a passionate kiss as Javier's fingers dance along my one-piece outfit, slowly and deliberately unfastening each button. The garment falls away, pooling at my feet. With trembling hands, I reach up to remove the pearl barrette from my hair, feeling my brunette curls tumble free across my shoulders and down my back.

Javier's lips blaze a trail of fire down the nape of my neck, sending shivers through my body. His hands move with practiced grace, sliding the straps of my bra over my shoulders. One hand massages and exposes my breasts while the other deftly unhooks the back clasp. In one fluid motion, my brassiere joins the growing pile of discarded clothing on the floor.

My eyes drink in every inch of Javier's form as I begin to undress him, my fingers working methodically to untuck and unbutton his starched Oxford shirt. As he shrugs it off, I move to his waistband, my heart racing as I undo the metal button and slowly lower the zipper. Javier steps out of his jeans, and we stand before each other, bare and vulnerable.

A silent conversation passes between us, our eyes speaking volumes that words never could. His finger traces a line down my spine, igniting sparks beneath my skin as he pulls me close until there's no space left between us.

With infinite tenderness, Javier cradles me in his arms and gently lowers me onto the bed. He lies down beside me, his lips finding my abdomen in a series of soft, reverent kisses. My breath catches as I watch his expression suddenly shift to one of concern.

"¿Que pasó?" Javier inquires, his voice laced with concern. His words send a jolt of panic through me as I realize what caught his attention.

Suddenly, a tidal wave of insecurities crashes over me, threatening to drown me in doubt and self-consciousness. My face burns with shame, thoughts spiraling wildly out of control. *Is he repulsed by the ugly scar from my high school surgery?* The jagged reminder of my past feels like it's searing my skin, leaving me raw and exposed.

My heart pounds frantically as I fight the urge to cover myself, to hide from his gaze. The scar, usually hidden and forgotten, now feels like a glaring imperfection, a mark of my damaged past. I'm overwhelmed by a crushing sense of inadequacy, feeling unworthy of Javier's affection.

The room suddenly feels too small, too intimate. I struggle to breathe, each inhale sharp and painful as I brace myself for rejection. The warmth and safety I felt in Javier's arms moments ago now seem like a distant memory, replaced by a cold, gnawing fear that threatens to consume me.

I nervously try to explain, stumbling over vocabulary that is still foreign to me. Without a dictionary, my explanation falls short, leaving me feeling exposed and vulnerable. Javier seems to sense my uneasiness, understanding without the need for translation. His eyes soften with compassion, making me feel both seen and terrified.

Overwhelmed by embarrassment, I slide under the comforter, desperately seeking shelter. *How could I have put myself in such a vulnerable position?* With nowhere to run or hide, I clutch the covers tightly around me, frozen in place, my body rigid with tension.

Gently, Javier pulls the comforter back down, exposing my midriff once more. He notices my stiff posture, the tension in my stomach muscles. With infinite care, he wipes away a tear from my cheek, cupping my face in his warm hands. "Me encantas tal y como eres (I like you exactly as you are)," he reminds me, his voice filled with sincerity and warmth.

His words wash over me like a soothing balm, slowly melting away the icy grip of my insecurities. "Estoy enamorado de ti (I am in love with you)," Javier whispers, his voice soft and sincere, filled with a depth of emotion that takes my breath away.

My heart swells with a rush of reciprocal feelings, both terrifying and exhilarating. "Yo también," I tell him, my voice barely above a whisper, thick with emotion. The words feel both foreign and familiar on my tongue, a declaration that changes everything and nothing all at once.

I can feel the weight of my worries begin to lift, evaporating like morning mist in the warmth of our shared affection. The connection between us is palpable, threads woven from shared moments and whispered confessions now becoming more tangible, more real.

I close my eyes, surrendering to the blissful sensation of being cherished, the joy of this realization washing over me like a warm, gentle rain, filling every corner of my heart with radiant light.

As I lay in Javier's arms, I feel wholeheartedly fulfilled and accepted, my earlier insecurities melting away in the face of his love. The realization crashes over me with startling clarity—I am in love with him too.

This feeling, so new and yet so familiar, wraps around me like a comforting blanket, making me feel safe, cherished, and completely alive.

My body tingles with an intoxicating blend of excitement and contentment, every nerve ending electrified and singing with pure, unbridled joy. In this perfect moment, time seems to stand still, suspended in a bubble of bliss. I wish I could freeze this instant forever, capturing the pure, unadulterated happiness that courses through my veins. I am loved, I am in love—and it's the most beautiful, terrifying, exhilarating feeling in the world.

"¿Por favor, quédate conmigo (Please, stay with me)?" Javier suggests, his voice a soft caress.

My heart leaps at his words, a kaleidoscope of possibilities unfurling before me. *Is he asking me to stay the night, or is this an invitation for something more profound?* A week, a month, or perhaps as long as it takes to discover if our love is truly everlasting? The thought makes my pulse race with a dizzying mix of hope and trepidation.

A wild, reckless idea begins to take root in my mind. Maybe I can find a way to extend my stay, to stretch this magical interlude into something more permanent. *Would it be completely absurd to misplace my airline ticket, or even my passport?* The notion is thrilling and terrifying in equal measure, a testament to the overwhelming power of this newfound love.

My mind races with possibilities, a whirlwind of hope and desperation. Without being completely irresponsible, there has to be a way to stay. My aspiration to be a teacher suddenly feels like a lifeline. The university here offers education degrees—I could finish my schooling here, couldn't I? My heart pounds at the thought of easily finding a job as an English educator, a perfect excuse to remain in this paradise I've grown to love.

Until I met Javier, I had no idea how it felt to be truly, deeply loved. The realization hits me like a tidal wave—*can I see myself seeking dual citizenship, or even relinquishing my own if need be?* The idea both thrills and terrifies me.

Of course, I would miss family and friends, the thought causing a pang of guilt to pierce my heart. *But what is the alternative?* The mere idea of missing Javier feels like a physical ache, a void I'm not sure I could ever fill.

Maybe, just maybe, Javier would be willing to emigrate to the United States? The hope flutters in my chest like a caged bird. But would he, could he truly embrace an American way of life? Doubt creeps in, clouding my vision of a perfect future together.

Can I even accept going back without plans for having him in it? The thought leaves me breathless, panic rising in my throat. The life I had before now seems colorless, devoid of the vibrant joy I've found here with Javier.

I'm torn between two worlds, my heart stretched across an ocean, yearning for a way to bridge the gap. The intensity of my emotions overwhelms me, leaving me dizzy with the weight of decisions that could alter the course of my entire life. In this moment, wrapped in Javier's arms, I feel both invincible and utterly vulnerable, ready to risk everything for love yet terrified of the unknown path ahead.

Burrowing my head on his chest, we lay entwined for the next hour, our bodies melding together as if afraid to let go. Every gentle caress, every soft breath feels like a precious gift, a moment to be treasured. Our fingers remain interlocked, a physical manifestation of our unwillingness to disconnect, even as Javier drives me across town.

The street is eerily quiet as we approach my home, the stillness broken only by the sight of the armed guard in the distance. My heart clenches, reality intruding on our bubble of bliss. As Javier pulls up in front of my gated home, time seems to slow, each second stretching painfully as we face our impending separation.

We engage in one last kiss, pouring every ounce of emotion into this final embrace. Javier's whisper of "Hasta la próxima vez" sends shivers down my spine, his words a lifeline of hope in the face of our uncertain future.

The finality I felt when saying goodbye to my university friends pales in comparison to the ache in my chest as I prepare to leave Javier. Yet his words, implying a 'to be continued,' ignite a spark of hope within me. Perhaps a long-distance relationship isn't just a dream, but a possibility we can nurture.

As we part ways, our promises to write and call feel like sacred vows. Each future letter and phone call will become a precious link, a way to keep our love alive across the miles that will soon separate us.

The weight of our emotions hangs heavy in the air, a bittersweet mixture of love, hope, and the pain of separation that threatens to overwhelm me as I watch Javier's car disappear into the distance.

Unable to fall asleep, I reach for my journal, hoping to pour out my swirling emotions onto its pages. As I open my bag, my breath catches in my throat at the sight of something unexpected. My fingers tremble as I pull out a business card, instantly recognizing it as Javier's.

With a pounding heart, I turn the card over, my eyes drinking in every word of Javier's handwritten message. Tears well up as I read his declaration that I am the most beautiful girl he has ever met—his "muñeca," his precious doll. His promise to write sends a thrill through me, and I clutch the card to my chest, overwhelmed again by the depth of his feelings.

Each word of his vow to remember me and our time together feels like a caress, warming me from within. I can almost feel his lips on mine as I read about the "big kiss on my beautiful little mouth" he's sending me off with. A bittersweet smile tugs at my lips as I read his playful reminder not to forget to send him magazines.

The final line takes my breath away—"an Ecuadorian Guayaquileño who loves me very much." Tears spill down my cheeks as the full weight of our separation hits me. I press the card to my lips, as if I could somehow transfer my own unspoken feelings back to Javier through this precious token.

In this moment, alone with Javier's words, I feel both incredibly loved and achingly lonely. The card is a tangible connection to the man who has stolen my heart, and I know I'll treasure it always.

My heart skips a beat as I discover a cassette tape nestled alongside Javier's card. With trembling fingers, I open the case, my eyes scanning the list of songs he's recorded.

I see "nuestra canción" marked as our song. The realization that I can't listen to it now, lacking a cassette player, fills me with a bittersweet ache. This tape, a piece of Javier's heart, will have to wait until I'm home, making the anticipation almost unbearable.

Gently, I tuck the precious business card into my journal, treating it like a fragile treasure. As I crawl back under the covers, Javier's words dance through my mind, each one a tender caress to my soul.

I close my eyes, reliving the whirlwind of events that have transformed my life. At the center of it all stands Javier, the charming, handsome Guayaquíleño who captured my heart by the bay and chose me to be his date. His vibrant, affectionate personality challenged my shyness and insecurities, coaxing me out of my shell. Now, I'm returning home with a confidence I never thought possible, my heart full and my spirit soaring.

Our relationship, so pure and intensely personal, feels like a beautiful dream. The speed at which we connected, the depth of our unconditional care, and the complete surrender of inhibitions seem almost inconceivable. Yet, the strength of our physical and emotional bond is undeniable, a force that has reshaped my world.

As sleep finally begins to claim me, I feel a profound sense of fulfillment washing over me. In this moment, wrapped in the warmth of Javier's love—even from afar—I feel complete. My last conscious thought is a prayer of gratitude for this unexpected, life-changing gift, and a hope that our connection will endure across the miles that will soon separate us.

July 13, 1993
A SUITCASE OF MEMORIES

The next morning, I find myself perched on the edge of my bed, a tidal wave of emotions crashing over me as cherished memories flood my mind. My heart constricts painfully as I recall the first day I entered this room, surrounded by unfamiliar faces and quivering with nervous anticipation. Now, ten weeks later, I'm saying goodbye to people who have become my family, the thought of leaving them behind causing a lump to form in my throat that threatens to choke me.

With trembling hands, I pack my bags for the last time, each item I tuck away feeling like a piece of my soul being torn away and stored. The weight of uncertainty crushes me as I wonder if I'll ever see these dear faces again. My chest tightens with a bittersweet mix of grief and overwhelming gratitude for the experiences we've shared.

As I roll my luggage into the hallway and pull my bedroom door shut, the soft click feels like the final, heart-wrenching period in a beautiful story. Tears well up and spill over, streaming down my cheeks as I lean against the closed door, overwhelmed by the realization that this transformative chapter of my life has come to an end. In this quiet moment, I allow myself to grieve for what I'm leaving behind, my body shaking with silent sobs.

Gathering what little strength I have left, I force myself to walk across the hallway, counting every step, desperately trying to stretch out these final precious moments before saying goodbye to the loved ones who welcomed me into their family. My heart races as I approach their door, knowing this is our last goodbye.

Peeking into the doorway, I'm struck breathless by the beautiful sight before me – Ramona, radiant and serene, breastfeeding their new little bundle of joy. Victor sits propped up beside her, gently caressing the tiny arm of their beautiful daughter. Cristina and Enrique are seated at the foot of the bed, their eyes glued to cartoons. The scene is so full of love and warmth that it makes my impending departure even more painful.

While I was visiting the Galápagos Islands, Ramona gave birth to a healthy baby girl. An emergency C-section was required due to excessive blood loss during delivery, leading to a brief hospital stay. Coincidentally, my last night with Javier was Ramona and Yesica's first night at home.

As soon as Victor sees me in the doorway, his face lights up with a tender smile. "¡Ven aquí, mi hija!" he calls, his voice filled with affection. Those simple words – "Come here, my child" – break the last of my composure. Tears flow freely as I step into the room, my heart simultaneously breaking and swelling with love for this family that has become my own.

As I walk into the room, my heart swells with a bittersweet mix of joy and sorrow. Ramona, radiant despite her recent ordeal, cradles little Yesica close. "¡Qué linda!" I whisper, my voice thick with emotion as I gently touch the tip of Yesica's tiny nose. When Ramona offers for me to hold the newborn, I accept with trembling hands, overwhelmed by the trust she's placing in me.

As Yesica is placed in my arms, a faint burp escapes her lips, and I can't help but chuckle softly. Eight pounds of pure innocence, she fits perfectly in my embrace. The sweet scent of jasmine-scented baby lotion envelops me, and I marvel at her chubby arms and legs, the delicate creases around her wrists and ankles. Ten perfect little fingers, ten tiny toes – a miracle of life in my arms.

Tears prick my eyes as I gently rock Yesica, my heart aching with the bittersweet irony of saying hello and goodbye in the same moment. Though her eyes are closed, I swear I see a hint of a smile on her angelic face. The weight of this precious life in my arms stirs a deep longing within me – a fervent hope that one day, I too will experience this indescribable love as a mother.

Overcome with emotion, I carefully hand Yesica back to Ramona, my vision blurring with tears. I reach out to embrace my host mother, my voice cracking as I whisper, "Muchas gracias por todo." Her gentle response of "Por supuesto, mi hija" breaks the last of my composure, and I find myself enveloped in a group hug as Cristina and Enrique join in.

I take pictures with my Ecuadorian family, each click of the camera capturing a piece of my heart I'll be leaving behind. Our promises to keep in touch feel almost inadequate given the profound bond we've formed, yet I cling to them like a lifeline, desperate to hold onto the connection that has brought so much warmth and love into my life.

The shout of "¡Vamos!" from downstairs shatters the moment, reminding me that my time here has truly come to an end. As I descend the tiled stairs, memories of Victor calling me his "gordita" flood my mind, bringing a bittersweet smile to my tear-stained face. Now he has his own little "gordita" to cherish.

With each step, I feel the weight of my experiences here, the love I've found, and the person I've become. As I reach my waiting father, I'm acutely aware that I'm not just leaving a country, but a piece of my heart and the girl I once was.

I climb into the van, my heart constricting painfully at the sight of Nilda and Juanita waving from the courtyard. Their figures grow smaller as we pull away, and I feel a piece of myself being left behind with them.

The absence of my beloved friend Mayra, called home to tend to her ailing mother, leaves an aching void. While I'm grateful for our earlier goodbye – knowing that parting on this day would have been unbearable – I can't help but feel the weight of her absence.

At the airport, my father and I embrace, the warmth of his arms around me both comforting and heart-wrenching. Memories flood my mind, transporting me back to the first night we met. I can almost hear his voice, perfectly crooning "Stand by Me" despite not knowing a word of English. That same spirit that endeared him to me then now threatens to overwhelm me with emotion, as I realize how deeply his influence has shaped my experiences here.

As the plane takes flight, my throat tightens and tears blur my vision. I cling to the hope that I'll return to Ecuador someday, even as a part of me knows it will never be quite the same. The realization hits me like a physical blow – nothing will ever be the same again. The girl who arrived here weeks ago is not the one leaving now, and the bittersweet ache of growth and change settles in my chest.

I press my forehead against the cool window, watching the landscape of my adopted home shrink beneath me. Each mile that passes feels like it's stretching the invisible threads connecting me to the people and places I've grown to love.

As Ecuador fades from view, I close my eyes, trying to imprint every memory, every smell, every emotion onto my heart. The future stretches before me, unknown and slightly terrifying, but I carry with me the strength and love I've found in this beautiful country.

July 19, 1993
SHARING STORIES

E ven before the fog of jet lag fully lifts, I find myself at the local pharmacy, my heart racing with anticipation as I drop off fifteen precious rolls of film. The wait for development feels interminable, each passing day heightening my longing to relive the memories. I order doubles of everything without hesitation; each image is a treasured link to the life I left behind.

Hours melt into days as I pour my heart into letters, each one a labor of love addressed to classmates, professors, and my beloved host family. My hand cramps from writing, but I barely notice, lost in the bittersweet joy of reliving shared moments and expressing my profound gratitude for their kindness.

When I finally receive the developed photos, my breath catches in my throat. There, frozen in time, are the faces of those who became my second family. I carefully select pictures to send to Mayra and my host family, each one chosen with care and accompanied by a piece of my heart.

The two pictures of Javier feel like precious gems, but the one of just the two of us makes my heart race with emotion. I decide to enlarge it to an 8x10 and place it in a vibrant pink multi-colored frame beside my bed.

Each night, as I drift off to sleep, his smile is the last thing I see—a bittersweet reminder of our deep emotional connection challenged by the physical distance between us. It's a constant reminder of the love we've shared, a love that transcends miles and time, filling my dreams with warmth even as I long for his presence.

Organizing my albums becomes a ritual, each page a carefully curated testament to my journey. As I arrange photos of Manabí, Quito, Otavalo, Cotacachi, and the Galápagos Islands, I'm transported back, feeling the warmth of the sun and hearing the laughter of newfound friends. My journaling becomes a cathartic outpouring of emotions, each word etched with love and nostalgia.

Sharing my experiences becomes a passion, my voice animated and my eyes shining as I recount tales of my home away from home. The shy girl who once dreaded public speaking has been replaced by a confident woman, eager to share the transformative power of her journey.

As word spreads and opportunities to present arise, I find myself standing before groups large and small, my voice steady and passionate. Whether I'm describing the humble beauty of thatched-roof huts in Manabí or the sophisticated architecture of Quito, I speak with newfound assurance, my words painting vivid pictures of the country that stole my heart.

In these moments, as I share my love for Ecuador with others, I feel closest to the person I became during my time there—confident, engaged, and filled with a zest for life and learning. Though an ocean away, Ecuador remains alive in my heart, shaping the woman I am becoming and fueling dreams of future adventures.

July 23, 1993
THE FIRST LOVE LETTER:
A JOURNEY BACK IN TIME

With a swirl of anticipation and nervousness in my chest, I set off on my quest to find the perfect men's fashion magazine for Javier. Each step feels electric with purpose as I navigate through various shops, my heart racing with hope. Finally, in a quaint specialty store tucked away in an unfamiliar neighborhood, I spot it. The salesclerk hands me *GQ Magazine*, its glossy cover featuring Arnold Schwarzenegger. "This one's a great choice for your friend," he says, and I can't help but smile at the thought.

My hands tremble slightly as I reach for the magazine, the weight of its significance making it feel heavier than it should. As I flip through the pages, a wave of excitement washes over me. Each stylish image and sophisticated article feels like a piece of American culture I can share with Javier, bridging the distance between us.

I can almost see his face lighting up as he receives each issue, his fingers eagerly tracing the contours of well-dressed models and sleek accessories. The thought of Javier poring over these pages, absorbing the fashion and lifestyle tips, fills me with a warm glow of connection.

As I leave the store, clutching the current issue to my chest, I'm filled with a mix of excitement and longing. This magazine represents so much more than just fashion—it's a way to keep our connection vibrant and alive. With each issue, I hope he'll feel my love and dedication reaching across the ocean, reminding him that he's always in my thoughts.

With shaking hands, I fill out the subscription card, my pen hovering over each blank as I imagine Javier's delight at receiving this bi-monthly slice of America. As I seal the envelope containing my payment, I feel like I'm sending a piece of my heart along with it. This small act feels monumental—a tangible link between Javier and me, a promise of shared experiences despite the miles between us.

With a flutter of excitement in my chest, I begin my first letter to accompany the magazine. "Querido Javier," I write, my heart racing as the words flow onto the paper. My pen dances across the page, driven by an overwhelming desire to connect with him across the miles. "None of the models in these pages are as handsome as you," I write, a warm blush spreading across my cheeks. I can almost see his playful smile as he reads these words, and it makes my heart skip a beat.

I pause, my fingers trembling slightly as I reach for the cherished photograph from our last night together. Carefully, I tuck it into the large manila envelope, imagining Javier's eyes lighting up when he sees it. "I'm enclosing a picture of us from our last night," I continue, my voice barely above a whisper as I read the words aloud. "I have the same photo beside my bed. It reminds me every day that I'm the luckiest girl in the world."

As I write, memories of our time together flood my senses. I can almost feel the warmth of his embrace, hear the sound of his laughter, and smell the familiar scent of his cologne. Tears prick at my eyes, a bittersweet mix of joy and longing that threatens to overwhelm me.

With each word, I hope that somehow, the depth of my feelings will transcend the physical distance between us. This letter is more than just ink on paper— it's a lifeline, a bridge across the ocean that separates us.

As I seal the envelope, I press a tender kiss to it, my lips lingering for a moment as I imagine Javier on the other side. I close my eyes, willing all my love and longing into this simple gesture, hoping that somehow, he'll feel the warmth of my affection when he holds this envelope in his hands.

This letter, this magazine, this photograph— they're all pieces of my heart that I'm sending across the miles. They're a testament to a love that knows no boundaries, a love that I hope will keep burning bright until we're together again.

I can't help but marvel at the cost—$12.29 to send this precious cargo to Ecuador. It's so much more than the simple letters I've sent to friends and family before, but then again, this is no ordinary correspondence. This package carries my hopes, my dreams, my love.

As I hand it over to the postal worker, I'm acutely aware of the journey it's about to undertake. Three to four weeks, they tell me, but it feels like an eternity. I imagine it soaring over oceans and continents, a tangible representation of my affection winging its way to Javier.

The thought of it passing through customs makes my stomach flutter with nervous anticipation. *Will they handle it gently? Will they understand the importance of what's inside?* I silently plead with unseen officials to treat it with care, to speed it on its way.

Finally, I picture it arriving at Javier's business post office box. My heart races at the thought of him holding this package, this piece of me, in his hands. *Will he feel the love I've poured into every word, every choice?*

As I walk away from the post office, I'm filled with a bittersweet mix of hope and longing. Three to four weeks suddenly seems like an impossibly long time to wait. But I comfort myself with the knowledge that soon, very soon, Javier will have a tangible reminder of my love, bridging the miles between us with the power of the written word and the depth of our connection.

August 2, 1993
NEW SCHOOL, NEW SEMESTER

My time at community college was invaluable, filled with growth and learning, but now I yearn to spread my wings. I'm excited about branching out, meeting new people, and discovering what the future holds for me. Each day feels like a blank canvas, waiting for me to paint my dreams upon it. The possibilities are endless, and I can almost feel the thrill of adventure calling to me, urging me to embrace the unknown. The sky truly is the limit, and I am ready to soar.

Corresponding with my roommate, Kassie, has been a mix of excitement and nervousness as we discuss who will bring what for our dorm room. We've exchanged ideas over the phone, eagerly planning how to make our shared space feel like home. The checklist of suggested items includes a few electronics and small appliances—things that aren't mandatory but would certainly enhance our college experience. While there's a lounge at the end of the hall with a TV, a small refrigerator, and a microwave, the thought of sharing that space with twenty or more girls is daunting.

Thankfully, I find solace in my mother's rescurcefulness. With her thrifty nature, she scours local consignment stores, strategically finding each small appliance for our room, easing my worries about the chaos of dorm life. Kassie insists on a coffee maker, even though I don't drink coffee, and adds it to her list of contributions. She also plans to bring a fan, an area rug, and a phone with an answering machine. We both decide to bring our own stereos and music—a choice I later realize was a stroke of genius.

As I think about our plans, I feel a mix of excitement and apprehension. This new chapter is filled with endless possibilities, and I can't help but wonder how we'll navigate the challenges and joys of dorm life together. The thought of creating memories in our shared space fills me with hope, and I'm ready to embrace every moment, no matter how chaotic it may be.

Over the next few weeks, my mother and I embark on a whirlwind of shopping trips, each one bringing me closer to the reality of leaving home. My heart flutters with a mix of excitement and nervousness as we pick out a new bedspread with matching sheets for my twin bed. The floral pattern I choose feels like a small piece of home I can take with me—a comfort in the unfamiliar world I'm about to enter.

When the saleswoman recommends a "boyfriend pillow" with arms, my cheeks flush as I immediately think of Javier. I can almost feel his arms around me, providing comfort as I study late into the night. The daydream is so vivid that I'm startled when my mother shakes my arm, pulling me back to reality. "Olivia, are you paying attention?" she asks, and I nod, trying to hide the emotions swirling inside me.

As we continue shopping, each item that lands in our cart feels like a stepping stone toward my new life. The storage bins represent the memories I'll make, the desk lamp symbolizes late-night study sessions, and the alarm clock reminds me of the independence I'm about to embrace. My heart swells with a mix of anticipation and fear as I imagine using these items in my new home away from home.

With each purchase, the reality of my impending departure becomes more tangible. I'm filled with a bittersweet mix of emotions—excitement for the adventures ahead, anxiety about the unknown, and a deep, aching love for the life and people I'm leaving behind. As I pack these new possessions, I'm not just preparing for college; I'm packing up pieces of my heart, ready to carry them into this new chapter of my life.

August 21, 1993
MOVE-IN DAY

As we arrive at the residence hall, I'm overwhelmed by the bustling energy around us. Cars line every inch of the sidewalk, and the air is thick with a mix of excitement and anxiety.

I watch as mothers and daughters struggle with overflowing laundry carts, their faces a blend of determination and barely concealed emotion. Fathers, boyfriends, and brothers grunt under the weight of electronics and appliances, each item a piece of home being transplanted into this new world.

My heart races as I approach the front desk to check in. The keys I'm handed feel weighty in my palm—not just metal, but symbols of my newfound independence. I'm officially a college student now, and the realization hits me with a rush of exhilaration and fear.

As we make our way to my room, I feel a knot forming in my stomach. Meeting Kassie and her family at the doorway, I put on a brave face, shaking hands and exchanging pleasantries. But inside, I'm a whirlwind of emotions. Seeing her side of the room already perfectly arranged makes me acutely aware of how unprepared I feel for this new chapter.

The moment of goodbye arrives all too soon, feeling like déjà vu. As my mother hugs me, her eyes brimming with tears, I feel my own emotions threatening to spill over. Her words of pride wrap around me like a warm blanket, and I cling to them, knowing I'll need that comfort in the days to come. My father's embrace, strong and steady, speaks volumes even without tears.

And then, in a heartbeat, they're gone. The sudden silence is deafening. I stand alone in my half-empty room, my chest tight with a mix of excitement, fear, and an overwhelming sense of loss. This is it—the beginning of my new life.

Turning to face my unpacked belongings, I take a deep breath, steeling myself for the journey ahead. On my own now, I'm ready to write the next chapter of my story, even as the bittersweet ache of what I'm leaving behind lingers.

With a mix of excitement and trepidation, I start organizing my side of the room. Each item I unpack feels like a piece of my heart settling into this new space. My style, an eclectic reflection of my journey and experiences, begins to take shape. I can't help but glance at Kassie's meticulously organized side, feeling a twinge of inadequacy.

With trembling hands, I hang the "Imagine" poster I bought from the bookstore. John Lennon's memorial, adorned with flowers, resonates deeply, symbolizing peace and possibility. Smoothing out the creases, I feel a connection to a world beyond these four walls.

Next, I carefully unfurl the handmade wool tapestry from Otavalo. As I hang it above my desk, my fingers linger on the intricate patterns. The images of indigenous people carrying children and crops transport me back to Ecuador, and I'm overwhelmed by a wave of nostalgia.

This piece of art, more than just decoration, is a window to a simpler, more grounded way of life that I've left behind.

With each photo I pin to my corkboard, my heart swells with love and longing. The faces of my pets, family, and friends—both from home and Ecuador—smile back at me, a patchwork of my life's journey. I blink back tears, realizing how far I've come and how much I've left behind.

Finally, with reverence, I place the framed picture of Javier and me from our final night together on my bedside desk. As I gaze at his warm smile, I can almost feel his gentle embrace and hear his loving words. A tightness forms in my throat as I realize that while I may feel lonely in this new territory, his presence in this photo will be my anchor, a reminder of the love and experiences that have shaped me.

Standing back, I survey my newly decorated space. It may not be as perfectly organized as Kassie's side, but it's uniquely mine—a tapestry of memories, dreams, and the person I'm becoming. In this moment, surrounded by pieces of my past and poised on the brink of my future, I feel a complex mix of homesickness, excitement, and hope for what lies ahead.

August 23, 1993
ROOMMATE ROULETTE

Settling into my new dorm room, I initially revel in the thrill of independence, but that excitement soon gives way to a heavy wave of disappointment and frustration. The freedom to come and go as I please feels hollow in the face of the overwhelming challenges I face daily.

My heart sinks every time I enter our cramped, shared space. Kassie, my roommate, might as well be from another planet. Her life as a former Homecoming and Prom queen, cheerleading captain, and girlfriend to her high school sweetheart feels like a stark reminder of how different we are. Each day, I feel more and more like an outsider in my own room.

Kassie's mood swings are like unpredictable storms, leaving me constantly on edge. Her spoiled nature and expectation of always getting her way grate on my nerves, making me feel small and insignificant. When she talks, her words are a torrent of self-centered chatter that drowns out any attempt I make to share my own experiences or thoughts.

The worst part is the wall of indifference she's built around herself. My stories of Ecuador, my dreams, my 'foreign' friends—all bounce off her like pebbles against a fortress. I feel my world shrinking, my experiences diminishing in value with each disinterested glance she throws my way.

Feeling a wave of loneliness wash over me, I decide to call Javier. We've only spoken twice since I returned to the States, but this will be the first time since moving into my dorm.

Sitting in the hallway with the phone cradled in my hands, my heart races with anticipation as it rings. When he finally answers, a rush of warmth envelops me, and I feel an overwhelming sense of relief. Hearing his voice offers security, wrapping around me like a comforting embrace and momentarily easing the deep loneliness that has settled in since I arrived.

"Olivia!" he exclaims, his excitement radiating through the line, and I can't help but smile, feeling a spark of joy amid my loneliness. As we talk, I savor the familiar cadence of his voice, each word a reminder of the connection we share.

But beneath the surface of our conversation, a worry gnaws at me. He doesn't mention the package I sent, and a pang of anxiety strikes my chest. I silently assume he hasn't received it yet; the thought of him missing out on the little tokens of my affection weighs heavily on my heart. I had poured so much love into that package, each item carefully chosen to remind him of our time together—a magazine to inspire him, and a picture from our last night together to capture the essence of our everlasting love.

As we continue to talk, I feel the weight of my loneliness lift just a little. Javier's laughter and the warmth of his words fill the void this new environment has created. In this moment, I am reminded that even though we are miles apart, our bond remains strong. Each conversation with him rekindles my spirit, igniting a flicker of hope that we can navigate this new journey together, no matter the distance.

As I open the door and return the phone to Kassie's dresser, the warmth of my conversation with Javier quickly evaporates. My heart sinks as I witness Kassie's dramatic display of disgust.

"Yuck!" she exclaims. The harsh sound of her aggressively wiping down our shared phone with a Clorox wipe pierces through me like a physical blow. Each swipe feels like a knife twisting in my gut, tearing away at the precious connection I just experienced. Her actions scream louder than any words could, making it painfully clear that she sees my relationship, my cherished connection to Ecuador, as something dirty and undesirable.

My cheeks burn with a mix of shame and anger as I watch her scrub away any trace of my conversation, and a lump begins forming in my throat as I struggle to hold back tears. This moment, which should have left me feeling loved and connected, now leaves me feeling small, insignificant, and utterly alone. The joy of hearing Javier's voice is tainted by the cruel reminder that in this new world, our love is seen as something to be cleansed away.

As Kassie continues her aggressive cleaning, I retreat to my side of the room, my heart heavy with the weight of her unspoken judgment. The promise of college life, of new experiences and growth, seems to be slipping away, replaced by a suffocating sense of isolation and misunderstanding.

I find myself longing for the warmth and acceptance I felt in Ecuador, wondering if I'll ever find that sense of belonging here in this cold, unwelcoming dorm room.

August 24, 1993
THE ALL-ACCESS PASS

In the dorms, privacy becomes a distant memory, a luxury I never knew I'd miss so desperately. My room feels like a fishbowl where I'm expected to live out every aspect of my life under the constant gaze and judgment of others.

The simple act of taking a shower becomes an anxiety-inducing ordeal. The thought of brothers and boyfriends visiting sends a shiver of discomfort down my spine. And the whispered stories of successfully sneaked-in overnight guests leave me feeling even more exposed, as if the walls themselves have eyes.

I wrap my robe tightly around me, clutching my shower caddy as I prepare for the long walk down the hallway. The thin layer of terrycloth feels painfully inadequate, leaving my bare skin exposed to the world.

With each step, my heart races, pounding in my chest like a frantic drumbeat. I'm hyper-aware of every glance, every whisper, real or imagined, and the sensation of being watched sends a shiver down my spine.

Hanging my robe on the hook outside the shower stall feels like shedding the last of my defenses. As I slip behind the flimsy curtain, I'm struck by a wave of discouragement. The sound of water running in multiple stalls reminds me that I'm never truly alone, even in this most private of moments. The fear of someone accidentally intruding on this sacred space leaves me constantly on edge, unable to fully relax.

Beyond the lack of privacy, the shared nature of the showers brings a new level of discomfort. The thought of others' hygiene habits, or lack thereof, fills me with a creeping dread. Donning shower shoes feels like arming myself against an invisible enemy, while the sight of hair-clogged drains turns my stomach.

In these moments of vulnerability and discomfort, an overwhelming wave of homesickness washes over me. I close my eyes and imagine the sanctuary of my bathroom at home, where a long, hot shower or a luxurious bubble bath was once a simple, everyday pleasure. Even my time in Ecuador, with its cold showers, seems like paradise compared to this. At least there, I had the luxury of privacy—a space that was wholly mine. Now, those memories feel like distant dreams, tantalizing and just out of reach.

As I navigate the shared spaces, always on guard and aware of others' presence, I find myself desperately yearning for just a moment of true solitude. The chaos of communal living leaves me feeling frayed and vulnerable. I long for a space where I can let down my guard, where I don't have to be constantly vigilant about my surroundings.

Yet, even as I struggle, a small part of me recognizes that this, too, is part of the growth I came here for. But in these moments of vulnerability, that knowledge offers little comfort. All I can do is close my eyes, take a deep breath, and hope that someday, somehow, I'll find a way to carve out a space for myself in this chaotic new place—a small corner of privacy and peace amidst the storm of dorm life.

August 27, 1993
DINING HALL ADVENTURES

Clutching my meal card, I feel a swirl of excitement and anxiety in my stomach. The dining hall looms across the street, a hub of social activity that both thrills and terrifies me. My parents' thoughtful purchase of a meal plan is greatly appreciated, but it's a daily reminder of how far I am from home-cooked meals and familiar faces.

The rhythm of mealtimes becomes a strange dance of social navigation. Breakfast with Sherry, a familiar face from high school, offers a comforting start to my day. Her invitation feels like a warm hug, reminding me that I'm not completely alone here.

Joining classmates for lunch and floor mates for dinner, I catch a glimmer of hope. Each shared meal offers a chance to build new connections and carve out my place in this vibrant community. But beneath the surface, a nagging worry persists. I watch as other roommates laugh together, sharing inside jokes and creating bonds that seem to grow stronger with each passing day.

In contrast, my relationship with Kassie feels like a chasm that widens with each awkward interaction. Our differences loom large, making even the simplest conversations feel like navigating a minefield. The easy camaraderie I see between other roommates is a painful reminder of what Kassie and I lack.

Each meal becomes a small act of courage. Despite the loneliness that sometimes threatens to overwhelm me, I hold onto hope. I remind myself that this is just the beginning, that friendships take time to develop, and that somewhere in this sea of unfamiliar faces, I will find my people.

August 30, 1993
INTERNATIONAL CONNECTION

While other girls indulge in shopping sprees and carefree purchases, I find my own obsession veering in a different direction—international calling cards. I find myself meticulously budgeting, sacrificing small luxuries that my peers take for granted, all to ensure I can afford these precious weekly connections.

The thrill of purchasing a new calling card sends a jolt of excitement through me, far surpassing any joy I might feel from buying new clothes or accessories. These small plastic rectangles have become my lifeline to Javier, a tangible connection to the world I left behind and so desperately miss.

Each week, I count down the days until our call, my heart fluttering with anticipation. As the moment finally arrives, my hands tremble slightly as I dial the familiar sequence of numbers. Though our conversations are brief, each carefully rationed minute feels like a treasure, stretching time itself as we bridge the vast distance between us.

"Aló," comes the answer, and my breath catches in my throat.

"¿Se encuentra Javier?" I ask, my voice barely above a whisper. Even though I know he lives alone, this formal request has become a cherished ritual, a small piece of Ecuador I carry with me.

"Ay, mi muñeca! ¿Cómo estás?" His excited response washes over me like a warm embrace, instantly melting away the loneliness that's been my constant companion.

Javier's voice brings a rush of warmth as he quickly tells me he received the package I sent him. "Si tuviera una sola flor por cada vez que pienso en ti, tendría un jardín," he says, his words wrapping around me like a tender embrace. (If I had a flower for every time I think of you, I'd have a garden.) His way with words never fails to leave me breathless, igniting a flicker of joy in my heart.

"Te extraño," we both say, those simple yet profound words exchanged during each conversation. It doesn't matter who says it first; the longing behind those words is honest, heartfelt, and unwavering. Each time we speak, the weight of our separation hangs heavy in the air, yet it's a shared burden that somehow brings us closer.

As I listen to him, I can almost picture the smile on his face, the way his eyes light up when he talks about our memories. The distance between us feels both vast and insurmountable, yet in these moments, it fades just a little. His voice pulls me back to the love we share, reminding me that no matter how far apart we are, our connection remains unbreakable.

When we finally say goodbye, the silence that follows is deafening, leaving me with a heart full of love and an ache that only the next call can soothe.

September 7, 1993
CAUSE FOR CONCERN

Watching Kassie's transformation after accepting her sorority bid, I'm swept up in a whirlwind of emotions. She's excited about joining, but there's a desperation in her that makes my heart ache. Though she's never been particularly warm towards me, I can't shake the growing knot of worry in my stomach as I watch her change.

The secrecy surrounding her new 'sisterhood' feels suffocating, even from a distance. Her eyes now hold a guarded look, as if she's always on the verge of revealing something forbidden. This air of mystery only amplifies my unease, leaving me with a gnawing dread about what's really happening behind closed doors.

But it's the physical changes that truly alarm me. Kassie's once vibrant presence is fading before my eyes, like a flower wilting in harsh sunlight. Her clothes hang looser each day, her cheekbones becoming more pronounced. It's painfully obvious that she's starving herself, and the realization hits me like a punch to the gut.

I find myself lying awake at night, haunted by the hollow look in her eyes as she desperately seeks acceptance from girls she barely knows. The Kassie I first met is disappearing, replaced by a shadow of herself who seems willing to sacrifice everything—her health, her identity, her very essence—just to belong.

Though we're not close, I'm overwhelmed by a desire to reach out, to shake her and make her see what she's doing to herself. But the invisible wall between us, built from her indifference and my insecurities, feels insurmountable. All I can do is watch, my heart heavy with a mix of concern, frustration, and a deep, aching sadness for the girl Kassie used to be and the one she's becoming.

The whispered rumors of sorority initiation rituals creep through the dorm, sending unsettling shivers down my spine. The idea of being compelled to stand naked, completely vulnerable while others scrutinize and point out perceived flaws is unimaginable—a profound violation of dignity.

I try to imagine the deep, lasting scars such an experience would carve into one's psyche. Just thinking about it fills me with an overwhelming urge to wrap my arms around myself, as if I could shield my body and soul from such cruelty.

Suddenly, my own scar from high school surgery feels like a neon light, drawing unwanted attention and judgment. What was once a mark of survival now feels like a target, a flaw that others might circle and ridicule.

In these moments, I'm acutely aware of my own vulnerability, and the thought of willingly subjecting oneself to such scrutiny for the sake of belonging seems unfathomable. Yet, as I watch Kassie and others eagerly pursue this path, I'm left feeling both bewildered and deeply saddened by the lengths some will go to find acceptance.

September 11, 1993
CULTURE SHOCK

Reluctantly agreeing to attend a few off-campus frat parties, I feel a mix of curiosity and apprehension churning in my stomach. The Victorian-style mansions, adorned with prominent Greek letters, stand before us like castles from an elite kingdom.

The preparation feels like a bizarre ritual. We spend hours transforming ourselves, teasing our hair to impossible heights and applying layers of makeup like war paint. As I squeeze into skin-tight jeans and throw on the required oversized t-shirt and flannel, I feel like I'm donning a costume, playing a part in a performance I don't quite understand.

Approaching the backdoor entrances, I'm struck by the bizarre scene. Swarms of underage students, eyes bright with anticipation, clutch their money like offerings to a secret society. The air thrums with excitement and nervous energy, and I feel my heart racing in response.

As I hand over my five dollars and receive the iconic red solo cup, a wave of unease washes over me. The dark, dirty basement swallows us whole, the air thick with the smell of stale beer and sweat. Loud music blasts from portable stereo speakers, the bass thumping like a heartbeat, amplifying my anxiety.

The crowd presses in around the keg, a writhing mass of bodies united in their pursuit of inebriation.

Strangers bond over shared cups and raucous cheers of "chug, chug, chug." The goal is clear—to lose yourself in the haze of alcohol and noise. But for me, unable to drink due to my liver condition, I feel like an outsider looking in on a world I can never truly be part of.

Clutching my empty cup like a shield, I navigate this unfamiliar territory with growing discomfort. The thought of asking for water seems laughable, so I play along, paying for a cup I'll never use. As I discreetly fill and exchange cups with my friends, I'm acutely aware of my role as an imposter in this alcohol-soaked scene.

In another room, the atmosphere crackles with energy as people gather around a table, engrossed in a game they call 'beer pong.' Ten solo cups filled with beer are arranged in a pyramid formation at both ends of the table, gleaming under the dim lights like colorful gems waiting to be claimed.

Teams take turns launching a ping pong ball across the table, their faces a blend of focus and exhilaration. The goal is simple yet charged with tension: to land the ball in one of the cups. Each successful shot is met with cheers and high-fives, while the defeated opponent grimaces, knowing they'll have to down the cup where the ball landed.

The stakes of the game seem trivial, yet they mask a deeper reality: the pressure to conform, to drink and partake in this chaotic revelry, to lose oneself in the haze of alcohol. I can't help but feel isolated as I stand on the periphery, acutely aware of my own choices and the weight they carry.

As the night wears on, I watch the transformation around me with a mixture of fascination and unease. The air becomes charged with wild, unpredictable energy. Laughter grows louder, touches linger longer, and the lines between friendship and something more begin to blur.

I watch the intoxicated revelers around me, their inhibitions lowered and judgment clouded. Memories of that terrifying night on the Galápagos Islands with Rico come flooding back, and a sickening realization hits me. *Is this how Rico saw me that night? Did my carefree attitude send the wrong signals?*

The thought makes me want to curl up and disappear, yet relief washes over me as I remember Rico stopping when I asked him to. *Thank goodness,* I think, my voice shaking even in my own mind. But that relief quickly turns into a deep, aching sadness. How close I came to a much worse fate. How easily it could have gone the other way.

As if the night couldn't possibly descend further into chaos, the harsh reality of these parties takes an even more disturbing turn. The need for basic human functions collides with the lack of proper facilities, and I watch with a mix of disgust and pity as partygoers stumble outside to relieve themselves. The sight of girls crouching behind cars or trees, desperately seeking a shred of privacy, makes my stomach churn.

Witnessing this demeaning scene, my thoughts suddenly drift to Mayra and the stories she shared about her village. I recall her descriptions of the challenging living conditions, where proper sanitation was a luxury many couldn't afford. In that moment, the stark contrast between two worlds hits me like a punch to the gut.

The villagers Mayra spoke of had no choice—their circumstances forced them to make do with limited resources. But here, at an institution of higher learning, these privileged students are willingly reducing themselves to such a degrading state. The bitter irony is almost too much to bear.

As I cautiously navigate the yard, my heart pounds in my chest. I try to avoid stepping in puddles of urine, feeling a potent mix of disgust and sadness.

September 27, 1993
ENGLISH CLASSES

As I settle in for our weekly call, my heart swells with anticipation. The moment Javier's voice comes through, I feel a rush of warmth and comfort wash over me.

"¿Cómo van tus clases, mi amor?" Javier asks, his voice filled with genuine interest. I can't help but smile, feeling a surge of excitement as I dive into describing my courses. When I mention my Spanish class, I hear the spark of enthusiasm in his voice, mirroring my own.

"¡Qué bueno! Cuéntame más," he encourages, and I feel a flutter in my chest. Talking about my favorite class with him feels so natural. Our conversation flows effortlessly, a beautiful dance of language and connection. I can't help but wish my professor could hear us, imagining the pride on her face if she could witness this real-world application of her lessons.

"If only I could get extra credit for this," I joke, feeling a bittersweet pang at the thought of how much more meaningful this practice is than any classroom exercise.

But then Javier surprises me with his own news. "Estoy tomando clases de inglés (I'm taking English classes)," he announces, his voice brimming with pride and excitement. My heart swells with emotion—love, admiration, and a fierce sense of pride all mingling together.

"¡Qué maravilloso!" I exclaim, genuinely thrilled for him. As he shares his experiences, his words tumble out in a rush of enthusiasm. It reminds me vividly of the little boys from my host family in Ecuador, their rapid-fire chatter filled with the joy of newfound knowledge.

Listening to Javier's eager attempts to practice his English, I'm transported back to those sun-drenched days in Ecuador. The memory is so vivid that I can almost feel the warmth on my skin and hear the laughter of those precious children. A lump rises in my throat—a mix of nostalgia and profound love for the man on the other end of the line.

As our call continues, I'm struck by the beautiful symmetry of our situations—both of us reaching across languages, cultures, and the vast distance that separates us. In this moment, our shared passion for learning and for each other makes the miles between us feel inconsequential.

Our conversation becomes more than just practice; it's a testament to our commitment, our growth, and the unbreakable bond we share. As we reluctantly say goodbye, I'm left with a heart full of love, pride, and a renewed determination to bridge the gap between us, one word at a time.

October 11, 1993
EL DÍA DE LOS MUERTOS

Sitting in Señora Reyes' classroom, I'm enveloped by a sense of excitement and wonder. Her passion for not just teaching the Spanish language but also sharing the rich culture of her Dominican heritage ignites a spark of interest within me. Each lesson feels like a journey, transporting me beyond the confines of our classroom walls to vibrant streets filled with the sounds and colors of a world I long to understand.

When Señora Reyes begins to talk about El Día de los Muertos, her eyes shine with excitement. I find myself leaning forward, hanging on her every word as she paints a vivid picture of this beautiful tradition. The contrast between the somber name and the celebratory nature of the holiday intrigues me, stirring a deep curiosity about how different cultures honor their departed loved ones.

As I absorb the information, my mind drifts to Javier and Ecuador. A surge of excitement courses through me as I realize I have a direct connection to another Spanish-speaking culture.

"¿Celebras Día de los Muertos en Ecuador?" I ask Javier.

"Sí, en Ecuador, se llama Día de los Difuntos," he responds.

More formally recognized as All Saints' Day, Halloween in the United States is a vibrant celebration where children don costumes and roam from house to house, eagerly asking for treats in a beloved tradition known as trick-or-treating. The memories of Halloween flood back to me, each one tinged with warmth and nostalgia. I can almost hear the laughter of my classmates and the rustle of costumes as we paraded around the school, prizes awarded for the scariest, funniest, and most creative outfits in each grade.

My mother, a talented seamstress, poured her heart into crafting costumes for my sister and me. We transformed into ladybugs, bumblebees, witches, and hobos, each outfit a testament to her creativity. Even before I traveled abroad or developed an interest in Spanish cultures, I distinctly recall dressing up as a Spanish señorita, my heart swelling with pride as I twirled in my colorful outfit.

"La señorita más hermosa que he conocido (The most beautiful señorita I ever met)," Javier says. Yet, I sense a hint of confusion in his tone. He doesn't quite grasp why I would choose to dress as a Spanish señorita when, in his culture, children and adults adorn themselves as skeletons, embodying the spirits of the dead.

While ghosts, mummies, and skeletons are popular choices among young boys in the U.S., often selected to elicit screams and shivers, the costumes in Latin American countries carry a deeper significance. With painted white faces, intricate black lines, and vibrant makeup accentuating their features, these outfits are a heartfelt tribute to the deceased.

I learn that, in Latin American cultures, it's believed that at midnight on October 31st, the souls of departed children descend from heaven, reuniting with their families. On November 1st, the spirits of deceased adults return to visit, creating a sacred connection between the living and the dead.

While both cultures celebrate with costumes and sweet treats, the essence of the festivities diverges dramatically. Instead of fearing the dead, Latinos embrace them, welcoming their loved ones back into their homes. They lovingly decorate altars with flowers and cherished trinkets, creating a space filled with memories. Some families host graveside picnics, feasting on their loved ones' favorite foods and returning home to indulge in a sweet bread dessert called pan de muerto.

Comparing these traditions to Halloween in the United States, I'm struck by a bittersweet realization. The familiar images of costumed children trick-or-treating suddenly seem shallow compared to the depth and meaning behind El Día de los Muertos and Día de los Difuntos.

A wave of gratitude washes over me—gratitude for Señora Reyes and her unconventional teaching methods, for Javier and the window he provides into Ecuadorian culture, and for this opportunity to expand my understanding of the world. I feel my perspective shifting and growing, and I'm filled with an insatiable hunger to learn more and dive deeper into the beautiful tapestry of cultures that make up the Spanish-speaking world.

October 13, 1993
GETTING A JOB

Staring at my dwindling funds, a knot of anxiety tightens in my stomach. My allowance from my parents is running out, and I know they won't indulge my obsession with international calling cards. The thought of losing my lifeline to Javier fills me with cold dread.

I can almost hear my father's voice, lecturing me about wasteful spending. The weight of his sacrifices presses down on me—all those business trips when Beth and I were younger, the careful budgeting to ensure our college education. His pride in providing for us without the burden of student loans was so important to him, and I feel a pang of guilt for wanting more.

Yet, beneath that guilt, a fierce determination persists. I know my father would view my spending on calling cards as irresponsible—a "premature charade," as he'd likely call it. The fear of his disappointment makes my heart race.

I can picture the look in his eyes, hear the sharp edge in his voice as he reminds me of his "high hopes" for his oldest daughter—hopes that certainly don't involve a 'foolish boy from South America.' My mother's well-meaning obliviousness—her assumption that Javier and I communicate primarily through letters—only adds to my inner turmoil.

But amidst this storm of emotions, a spark of hope ignites as I spot a job listing for the nearby grocery store. Memories of my high school job as a clerk flood back, bringing a sense of pride and independence. As I apply and ace the interview, I feel a surge of empowerment. This job is more than just a paycheck—it's my ticket to freedom, my chance to maintain my connection with Javier on my own terms.

With each shift I work, I feel a mix of emotions. There's satisfaction in being the perfect employee, knowing I'm valued for my accuracy and reliability. There's relief in escaping my roommate and the social pressures of dorm life. But underlying it all is a fierce, burning hope—every dollar I earn brings me one step closer to returning to Ecuador, to Javier.

October 23, 1993
HOMECOMING WEEKEND

H omecoming weekend is a magical time when the school and community unite in a vibrant display of pride and spirit. The air buzzes with excitement as parades wind through the streets, cookouts fill the air with the tantalizing aroma of grilled food, and the anticipation of the Saturday afternoon football game electrifies the atmosphere. It's a celebration that brings together university faculty, alumni, and current students, creating a rich tapestry of connections and camaraderie.

As one of my professors puts it, for seniors, this weekend is a chance to see and be seen—a pivotal moment in our college journey. Introductions within certain departments can lead to internships and job opportunities, making this weekend not just a celebration but a strategic networking event that could shape our futures.

The university thoughtfully invites alumni to speak at various engagements throughout the weekend, their testimonies filled with intention and heartfelt reflections. They share stories of their time here, expressing gratitude for being accepted into this institution. Their words serve as a powerful affirmation, reminding us that each successful student made the right choice in selecting this school as their alma mater.

Among the most impressionable guests are the families of underclassmen, and my own family is no exception. My father, an avid football fan, embodies the spirit of the weekend. Long before my sister Beth and I joined the marching band, he was cheering for our high school under the Friday night lights. With two players from our hometown on the university team, it's only fitting that he wants to be part of the fanfare, his enthusiasm infectious.

My mother's voice echoes in my mind as she urged my father to book our accommodations early. But, as usual, her reminders fell on deaf ears. I can almost hear her sighs of frustration as she watched him procrastinate, convinced everything would work out in the end.

Now, as the reality sets in that he's finally ready to look for a place to stay overnight, the harsh truth hits us: there are no vacancies left. Rather than spending the weekend together, they'll just have to come and go in one day.

A wave of disappointment washes over me, but I quickly push it aside. *Perhaps it's for the best*, I tell myself. This way, I can still work Friday night and Sunday morning, keeping my commitments intact.

November 2, 1993
A LOVE LIKE OURS

With Señora Reyes introducing us to West Side Story, my heart flutters with anticipation. The familiar strains of music fill the classroom, and I'm instantly transported to a world of forbidden love and cultural clashes. As the story of María and Tony unfolds on screen, I find myself holding my breath, my own love story with Javier playing out in parallel in my mind.

The similarities between María and me hit like a tidal wave of emotion. We're both young, naive, and unexpectedly swept off our feet by love that defies cultural boundaries. Watching María transform from a shy, obedient girl into a woman of fierce determination fills me with pride and recognition. This is my journey too, I realize—my own metamorphosis reflected in her story.

When María sings "I Feel Pretty," my mind drifts back to that magical first date with Javier. The memory washes over me, warm and intoxicating. I remember the butterflies in my stomach and how his eyes lit up when he saw me.

In that moment, just like María, I felt invincible, beautiful, chosen. As I recall how Javier made me feel that night—like the most cherished girl in the world—an overwhelming sensation rises within me.

As María and Tony's eyes meet on screen, I'm struck by the power of a single glance. I think of Javier's eyes, how they seemed to see into the depths of my soul. My heart races, remembering how a simple look from him left me breathless, uninhibited, completely myself.

With each scene, I'm back in Ecuador, reliving our most intimate moments. His acceptance of my scar, his gentle touch that made me feel beautiful despite my insecurities—it all comes rushing back. Tears prick my eyes as I remember the intensity of our last night together, the way he loved every part of me without hesitation.

As the final notes of "Somewhere" fade away, I'm left with a whirlwind of emotions—hope, fear, longing, and an unwavering determination to fight for our love, no matter the obstacles. Like María, I've been transformed by love, and I know in my heart that Javier and I will find our way back to each other, somewhere.

November 15, 1993
CROSSING BORDERS, FACING BARRIERS

Javier's determination to reunite with me in the United States fills me with both hope and anxiety. The process is daunting; it requires more than just a passport—he needs a visa to enter the country. As his sponsor, I, Olivia Weber, must vouch for him. Our relationship? Well, I'm his *novia*, his girlfriend, a word that carries all the weight of our love and longing.

Javier's visit is meant to be a simple act of tourism, but for us, it's so much more. It's a chance to close the gap that's been a constant ache in our hearts. The idea of finally seeing him, of having him here in my world, fills me with a joy that is almost overwhelming.

Yet, beneath the excitement, there's a thread of fear. What if something goes wrong? What if the visa is denied? The uncertainty gnaws at me, a reminder of how fragile our plans can be. But I hold onto hope, clinging to the belief that love will find a way.

Javier's voice trembles as he delivers the devastating news—his visa was denied. The words hit me like a physical blow, knocking the air from my lungs. In an instant, all our hopes and dreams come crashing down around us.

My heart races as I struggle to process this cruel reality. The excitement that had been building within me turns to ash, leaving a bitter taste in my mouth. I want to scream, to rage against the unfairness of it all, but I'm paralyzed by the weight of our shattered plans.

Questions flood my mind: *Why? What went wrong? How could they not see how much this means to us?* But I know there are no satisfying answers, just the cold, impersonal mechanics of bureaucracy that have deemed our love insufficient.

As the initial shock subsides, a fierce determination takes root. This setback, as crushing as it is, cannot be the end of our story. We've come too far and fought too hard to give up now.

Through his tears, Javier vows to try again. His resolve is both heartbreaking and inspiring, a testament to the strength of our love and the lengths we're willing to go to be together. Despite the obstacles, his determination rekindles my hope, reminding me that our journey isn't over. We'll face this challenge together, fueled by the belief that love will ultimately find a way.

When I left Ecuador, Javier gifted me a cassette of the album *Falta Amor* by the Mexican band Maná, a gesture that spoke volumes about his affection. Among the tracks, "Buscándola" became *our song*, a melody that encapsulated our bond. I listened to it so often that the tape began to wear thin, the ribbon inside threatening to snap and leave me with silence where our song once played. Fearing this loss, I replaced the cassette with a CD, ensuring the music would always be with me.

No matter my mood—whether joyful or sorrowful—this song wraps around me like a comforting embrace. Its blend of Latin pop, calypso, and reggae never fails to lift my spirits, compelling me to dance or sing along freely.

The translated lyrics, "Looking for Her," tell the poignant tale of a man, love-stricken and relentless in his search for his beloved across the globe. He journeys through Europe, Asia, and the Middle East, resisting temptations along the way, driven by an unwavering need to reunite with her.

This narrative resonates deeply with me, mirroring the longing I feel for Javier. The thought of him missing me with such intensity is both heartwarming and heartbreaking. As the music plays, I'm reminded of our connection and the hope that, like the man in the song, we will find our way back to each other, no matter the distance that separates us.

WHEN HOPE MEETS RED TAPE

I n my Cultural Anthropology class, excitement swells within me as we dive into the section on Latin America. The few short paragraphs dedicated to Ecuador in our textbook ignite a spark of familiarity. It feels as if a piece of my heart has found its way into our textbook, and I'm eager to breathe life into those brief words.

When Dr. Stevenson reveals that he also studied in Ecuador, I feel an instant connection. As he projects slides of the Andean region of Cuenca, I'm transported back to the breathtaking landscapes I visited during one of our weekend excursions. Each image stirs a whirlwind of emotions and memories within me.

The mention of cuy brings a bittersweet smile to my face. While I couldn't bring myself to try it, I remember the enthusiasm with which Ecuadorians recommended it. As my classmates cringe at the thought of eating guinea pigs, my heart sinks. I want to shake them, to make them see beyond this one aspect and appreciate the rich tapestry of Ecuadorian culture that I've come to love.

Dr. Stevenson shares a photograph of himself cradling a beautiful infant, and my heart instantly swells with warmth. The child's chubby cheeks and big brown eyes remind me of the kids my host mother drove to school, radiating pure innocence and joy. I find myself completely drawn in, unable to look away.

A smile spreads across my face as I feel an unexpected connection to this little one I've never met, as if their spirit is reaching out to touch mine, bridging the gap between us in a moment of pure, unfiltered love.

He then gently directs our attention to the child's foot. The moment I see the clubfoot condition, a tidal wave of emotions crashes over me. My throat tightens and tears prick at my eyes as I take in the twisted shape of the tiny foot.

The subsequent discussion about the prevalence of this condition in "third-world countries" like Ecuador stirs a complex mix of emotions within me. I feel a fierce protectiveness toward the country I've come to love, coupled with a deep sadness for the challenges faced by its people. The term "third-world" irks me, seeming overly simplistic and disrespectful to the vibrant culture and resilience I experienced firsthand.

As Dr. Stevenson delves into the nature vs. nurture debate surrounding clubfoot, I find myself hanging on every word, desperate to understand more about the country that has captured my heart. His explanation of how people in the region adapt to such challenges fills me with profound respect for their resilience, while igniting a burning desire to help, to make a difference somehow.

Dr. Stevenson continues to share his story, and I find myself completely captivated. The way he reached out to his fraternity brother, who then connected him with a medical professional, feels like a beautiful chain of human kindness. I'm in awe of how quickly people can come together to help a child in need.

When he describes the percutaneous transverse Achilles lengthening procedure, I feel a strange combination of fascination and queasiness. The idea of making a small cut in the Achilles tendon makes me wince, but the simplicity and effectiveness of the procedure fill me with hope. Fifteen minutes to change a child's life forever—it seems almost miraculous.

However, as Dr. Stevenson delves into the complexities of bringing the child to the United States for treatment, I feel a surge of frustration and anger. The bureaucratic hurdles, the need for sponsorship, the questioning of relationships—it all seems so cold and impersonal in the face of a child's urgent medical needs. The fact that Dr. Stevenson had to become the child's godfather just to facilitate her treatment both warms my heart and infuriates me at the system's rigidity.

The financial burden Dr. Stevenson took on—paying for travel expenses, hiring a lawyer, putting up thousands of dollars as a safeguard—leaves me in awe of his commitment. Yet, it also fills me with a sense of injustice. *Why should helping a child in need be so complicated and expensive?*

As Dr. Stevenson concludes his story, I'm overwhelmed by a tidal wave of emotions. My heart swells with inspiration, marveling at the incredible lengths people like him will go to help others. The selflessness and dedication he's shown fill me with a sense of awe and renewed faith in humanity.

Yet, alongside this warmth, a fierce anger burns within me. The systemic barriers that make such help so difficult to provide ignite a frustration that threatens to consume me. I clench my fists, fighting back tears of rage at the thought of bureaucracy standing in the way of changing lives.

But then, a tiny spark of hope flickers in my chest. As I think about Javier's denied visa, I can't help but wonder if Dr. Stevenson might have some insight to offer. My heart races with anticipation—*could this be the key to unlocking the door that's been slammed shut in our faces?*

As the other students file out of the classroom, my heart pounds in my chest, a thunderous rhythm echoing through the empty room. I linger behind, my palms clammy and my throat dry as I wait for my chance to speak with Dr. Stevenson.

During our private conversation, the realization dawns on me, and my heart sinks like a stone. The innocence of our love, once so pure and uncomplicated, now feels tainted by bureaucratic technicalities. I can't help but let out a bitter laugh, tinged with frustration and regret, as I think about how our use of "novia" might have inadvertently complicated everything.

The word "novia" now feels like a double-edged sword, cutting through our dreams of reunion. Its multiple meanings—girlfriend, fiancée, bride—swirl in my mind, each one a painful reminder of how our relationship defies simple categorization. We're more than just boyfriend and girlfriend, yet not quite engaged or married. The complexity of our love seems impossible to capture in a single word, let alone on a cold, impersonal visa application.

Tears of frustration sting my eyes as I think about the denied visa and another one just submitted for review, each rejection a blow to our hopes and his wallet.

The application fees weigh heavily on my conscience, representing not just money spent, but dreams deferred. I clench my fists, anger bubbling up inside me at the unfairness of it all.

With a heavy sigh, I whisper the word "amiga" to myself. It feels so inadequate, so painfully insufficient to describe what Javier means to me. Yet, I can't help but wonder if this simple word might have been our key to success. The thought leaves a bitter taste in my mouth, a stark reminder of how love can be reduced to semantics in the eyes of the law.

December 15, 1993
HOME FOR THE HOLIDAYS

The fall session has finally come to an end, and a wave of relief washes over me as I reflect on the hard work that has led to this moment. My heart swells with pride as I prepare to share the news with my parents during the drive home for the holidays: I made the Dean's List!

As we drive through the familiar streets, I can't help but daydream about the break ahead. Yes, it will be a time to relax, but more than anything, I can't wait to spend time with my best friend, Melanie. She is my rock, my confidante—the one person who truly understands the whirlwind of emotions I experience as I navigate my relationship with Javier.

Ironically, while I've been falling deeply in love with an Ecuadorian, Melanie has found herself smitten with a Puerto Rican named Marco, whom she met at the nightclub where she works as a cocktail waitress. We're both exploring love in different forms, and I can't wait to share our stories, our laughter, and our dreams during this much-anticipated break.

After a long yet fulfilling day of holiday shopping, the time has finally come to head home. No trip to the mall would feel complete without stopping for a picture with Santa. Even though Melanie and I are clearly too old to present our wish lists to jolly old St. Nick, we can't resist the charm of a Polaroid snapshot.

As we pose together, I can't help but feel a rush of nostalgia—a bittersweet reminder of the magic of childhood. The laughter and joy of the moment wrap around us like a warm blanket, but deep down, I know that, short of a Christmas miracle, my own wishes are unlikely to come true this year.

Melanie's mother is working late, so we've already made plans to order a pizza and rent a movie. Surveying the selections at Blockbuster, I assume we'll binge-watch a beloved coming-of-age film like *Sixteen Candles*, *Pretty in Pink*, or *Dirty Dancing*. However, while browsing the drama section, the words "forbidden dance" catch Melanie's eye.

"Wait a minute. Check this out," she says, pointing.

The plot summary on the back of the case describes the movie as: *A princess from the Amazon rainforest tries to fight a conglomerate threatening the forests by going to Los Angeles. There she links up with a rich kid who tells her that she must get on TV to succeed with her mission. The two come up with the idea of winning a lambada dance contest that is getting TV attention.*

The provocative tagline and steamy cover image ignite a spark of curiosity. Without hesitation, we decide this will be our evening's entertainment, and I can feel a giddy energy building between us.

As we watch the film, I'm transported back to Ecuador, the lush beauty of the Amazon rainforest vivid in my mind. A pang of sadness hits me as I realize Melanie doesn't seem to grasp the environmental message—her small-town upbringing evident in her indifference. I feel a momentary disconnect from my friend, wishing she could understand the importance of preserving such natural wonders.

When we attempt to mimic the lambada, my heart races with a mix of excitement and embarrassment. The dance steps bring back a flood of memories—salsa and merengue in Ecuador, Javier's warm hands guiding me, the rhythm of the music pulsing through my veins.

But this feels different—more intimate, more daring. I can feel the heat rising in my cheeks as I remember the confidence Javier instilled in me, yet the thought of being so overtly sensual still makes me blush furiously.

"I have an idea," Melanie says, her eyes sparkling with mischief.

"What?" I ask, my curiosity piqued.

"Let's call him," she suggests, and my heart leaps into my throat.

It's nine o'clock there, and I'm sure he's still up. *Why not?* The thought sends a thrill of excitement through me, mixed with a touch of nervousness.

With trembling fingers, I dial the number I know by heart. As the phone rings, I can feel my pulse quickening, anticipation building with each passing second.

But from the moment Javier answers, I can sense something is off. The usual warmth in his voice is replaced by a heavy, somber tone that sends a chill down my spine. My excitement quickly turns to dread as I realize he's very upset.

"What's wrong?" I ask, my voice barely above a whisper.

His words hit me like a physical blow. He was going to wait until after the holidays to tell me, but his second visa has been denied. The world seems to tilt on its axis as the weight of his words sinks in. All our hopes, our dreams of reunion, come crashing down around me.

The joy and playfulness of moments ago evaporate, replaced by a crushing sense of despair. Tears well up in my eyes as I struggle to find words—any words—to respond. The distance between us, once just a temporary obstacle, now feels like an insurmountable chasm.

As I clutch the phone, my knuckles white with tension, I'm overwhelmed by a tidal wave of emotions—anger at the unfairness of it all, heartbreak at the thought of more time apart, and a fierce determination to find a way, any way, to be together again.

March 5, 1994
UNRETURNED CALLS,
UNSPOKEN WORDS

I t's raining outside, the steady rhythm of droplets tapping against the window, mirroring the storm of emotions within me. While everyone else has headed downstairs for karaoke, I've chosen to stay back and study. I'm not quite sure what made me think I could focus on my work; my mind has been wandering for weeks, and my declining grades show that struggle. Socializing and having fun feel even more daunting right now.

So, I sit here at my desk, staring at the picture of our last night together, one hand propped against my forehead and the other resting next to the silent phone, willing it to ring with Javier's number. Nearly three months have passed since our last conversation, but the memory of that painful call is still raw. The ache of his absence gnaws at me, making it impossible to concentrate.

I had been so hopeful, so sure that Javier's second visa application would be approved. But when I called, his voice thick with emotion, I knew something was wrong. The consular officer had denied his request again.

"I can reapply in a year," he told me, regret heavy in his tone.

A year? My heart sank. I couldn't possibly wait that long. The past six months had been agonizing enough.

I miss everything about him—the way his cologne lingers in the air after he leaves, his infectious laugh, the warmth and safety of his strong embrace. Most of all, I miss how he makes me feel—like the most beautiful girl in the world.

Our whirlwind romance had been the most genuine and passionate connection I had ever experienced. We promised to make our long-distance relationship work, but I never anticipated how challenging it would be to reunite back in my homeland. Deep down, I know I should never have left; staying would have made everything easier.

My professor warned me, but I chose to ignore the signs. Identifying me as Javier's sponsor could imply he might try to overstay if temporary status was granted. What ties did he have to guarantee he would return to his home country if the woman he loved was American and lived in the U.S.?

I feel like a fool for not listening, for letting my heart overrule my head. I'd been so caught up in my desperation to see him that I forgot the real challenges we faced.

I've spent countless nights replaying our conversation, wishing I could turn back time and change the outcome.

"Then I'll find another way," Javier vowed, determination in his voice.

Another way? But how?

As if the delayed reunion weren't enough, he now isn't returning my phone calls. *If he truly loves me, then why isn't he picking up?*

My mind races with doubts and fears. *Maybe he's lost interest. Maybe the distance and struggle to reunite are too much. Maybe he's met someone else. Maybe there's always been someone else.*

The rain continues to fall, each drop a reminder of the uncertainty and longing that fills my heart.

Pushing those insecurities aside, I square my shoulders, steel my nerves, and carefully dial the memorized international phone number, 0-1-1-5-9-3-4...

The line begins to ring, a series of harsh tones cutting through the silence of my room. With each passing ring, my heart races faster.

Beep... Beep... Beep...

This time, I promise myself. This time, if he answers, we'll find our way back to each other, no matter what obstacles stand in our way.

Beep... Beep... Beep...

As the ringing continues, I close my eyes and whisper, "Please, Javier... I need to hear your voice. I need you."

Beep... Beep... Bee—

The harsh tones are abruptly cut off as the line connects with a sharp click.

"¿Aló?"

Startled by the muffled sound of a woman's voice, I quickly hang up the phone, my heart pounding. I must have dialed the wrong number.

Taking a deep breath, I try the number again, but the same unfamiliar voice greets me once more.

I swallow hard and ask in Spanish, "Is Javier there?"

My mind is reeling, struggling to make sense of the stranger's words on the phone. The only phrase I can grasp is "El murio," and it sends a chill down my spine.

Is... is she telling me he died? My heart pounds so loudly I can barely hear my own thoughts. *No, that can't be right. I must be misunderstanding.*

I clutch the phone tighter, my palms sweaty and my breath coming in short gasps. *What exactly is she trying to say?* I strain to catch any other familiar words, anything that might contradict the terrible meaning I fear.

A part of me wants to believe this is a cruel joke, a misunderstanding—anything but the truth. But the somber tone, the gravity in the stranger's voice... it all feels terrifyingly real.

This can't be happening. My mind is spinning with denial and disbelief. *Not Javier. Not now. Please, let this be a mistake.*

I feel like I'm drowning, struggling to stay afloat in a sea of confusion and fear. The words "El murio" echo in my head, each repetition driving despair deeper into my heart. I want to scream, to deny it, to wake up from this nightmare. But the stranger's voice continues, relentless, as I stand frozen, my world crumbling around me with each passing second.

Panic-stricken, I hang up on the woman again. It's all too much to process. My mind is racing, and I can feel my heart pounding in my chest. I can't breathe. I can't think. This can't be happening.

Hysterically crying, I fumble with my phone, desperately dialing Angelina's number. She's a girl from one of my classes last semester, and her family is from Puerto Rico. She speaks Spanish fluently. I need her help. I need someone who can understand what's being said.

My hands are shaking so badly I can barely hold the phone. I know Angelina is working the front desk at her dorm this weekend. I pray she'll answer. When she picks up, I can barely form coherent words through my sobs. I'm not even sure if she understands me, but I beg her to come to my room.

When Angelina arrives, I feel a small glimmer of hope. With trembling fingers, I dial Javier's number for the third time. As the female voice answers, I hand the phone to Angelina, holding my breath.

I watch Angelina's face intently as she speaks calmly in Spanish. My heart races, and I cling to the last shred of hope that this is all a misunderstanding. But as Angelina's expression changes, I feel my world crumbling around me.

When she turns to me, her eyes filled with sorrow, I know before she even speaks. "I'm so sorry, Olivia," she says softly. "Javier... he's gone."

The words hit me like a physical blow. I collapse to the floor, my body wracked with sobs. It feels like my heart is being torn from my chest. Javier is gone. My love, my future, my everything—gone.

Through my haze of grief, I vaguely hear Angelina explaining that the woman wouldn't or couldn't give any more details about his death. But it doesn't matter. Nothing matters anymore. My world has shattered, and I'm left drowning in a sea of pain and disbelief.

March 12, 1994
IN SEARCH OF ANSWERS

I need answers, but how am I going to find them? My host family doesn't know Javier, and I have no contact with his family or friends. The uncertainty gnaws at me, leaving a hollow ache in my chest. *Could there have been something published in a newspaper? At least an obituary? But where would I find a newspaper from Ecuador?* The only place that comes to mind is the Library of Congress in Washington, DC. It's a long shot, but it's the only lead I have.

With no time to delay, Angelina and I both call off work for the upcoming weekend. My heart pounds with a mix of desperation and determination. We have to find out what happened. Angelina, a member of AAA, suggests we visit a local agency for roadmaps. The kind gentleman behind the counter highlights the routes for us, and I feel a flicker of hope amid the chaos.

As we prepare for the journey, emotions whirl within me—fear of what we might discover, hope for answers, and a deep longing for closure. The road ahead seems daunting, but I know I have to take this step. For Javier, for myself, for the love that still burns brightly in my heart.

Sneaking out of Angelina's RA suite in the early morning darkness, my heart pounds with a mix of determination and fear. I'm grateful for her private room—it made our secret departure easier. We retrieve my car from the parking lot by the football stadium field house, and as we begin our journey, a surge of hope mingles with dread.

The three-and-a-half-hour drive feels both endless and too short. We only stop once, and I'm torn between wanting to arrive quickly and dreading what we might find. As we pull up to the Library of Congress just after ten, my stomach is in knots.

Entering the massive building, I'm immediately overwhelmed. The sheer size and grandeur make me feel small and lost. Tears well up in my eyes, threatening to spill over. But Angelina, bless her, takes my hand and pulls me toward the circulation desk. Her touch grounds me, reminding me why we're here.

"Come on," she says firmly, "no time for tears right now." I swallow hard and nod, clinging to her strength.

When the library assistant helps us identify the two major Ecuadorian newspapers—El Telégrafo and El Universo—I feel a glimmer of hope. But as we scan through countless articles on microfilm, that hope begins to fade. Each minute without finding anything about Javier feels like a knife twisting in my heart.

After hours of fruitless searching, I'm completely defeated and utterly exhausted. The weight of our failure presses down on me, making it hard to breathe. But I can't give up. I have to know what happened to Javier.

As we prepare to leave, empty-handed and heartbroken, I steel myself for the long drive back. We can't afford a hotel, and honestly, I doubt I could sleep anyway. Every mile back to school feels like we're moving further from answers, from Javier. But I keep driving, fueled by a desperate need to fill the aching void left by his loss and the questions that still haunt me.

March 15, 1994
OVERCOME WITH GRIEF

Kassie moved into the sorority house, so I have a new roommate for the second semester. Emily is more compatible—she's simple, down to earth, and an accounting major who studies all the time. I feel a sense of relief having a roommate who's less judgmental and more focused on her life.

I confide in Emily that someone very close to me died, but I hesitate to share more. The memory of Kassie's judgment still stings, and I can't face that again. Emily listens politely, but I can tell she's preoccupied with her studies. She has no idea how much this loss has affected me—how it's eating away at my very soul.

I find myself calling off work more often until I finally resign from my clerk position at the local grocery store. *What's the point of working anymore?* I no longer need money for international calling cards or to save for a reunion with Javier. The thought of him sends a fresh wave of pain through my heart.

Emily keeps inviting me to the dining hall with her friends, but I decline each time. The truth is, I'm not going at all. The thought of food turns my stomach, and I can feel myself getting thinner. But I can't bring myself to care.

Instead of going to classes, I lie in bed all day, staring at the ceiling. The world outside my dorm room feels distant and unreal. Showers become a monumental effort, quick and routine whenever I manage to take one at all. My grades are slipping, but it feels meaningless now. I drop two classes just before getting a mid-term failing notice, but the relief is hollow.

I've lost all interest in things that used to matter. My textbooks gather dust; my word processor sits untouched. Nothing seems to matter anymore. I've cried so much that I don't even have tears left. This isn't just sadness—it's a deep, suffocating depression that's taken hold of me.

The weight of Javier's loss presses down on me constantly. Every moment feels like I'm drowning, struggling to breathe in a world that suddenly makes no sense. I know Emily notices something's wrong, but she doesn't know how to help, and I don't know how to ask. I'm adrift in a sea of grief, and I can't see any shore in sight.

March 17, 1994
DROWNING IN DESPAIR

The phone rings in the middle of the afternoon, and I see Angelina's name on the caller ID. My heart sinks, knowing she's probably checking up on me.

"Hey Liv, ¿Cómo estás?" her cheerful voice comes through the line.

"Así, así," I mumble, trying to sound more okay than I feel.

I can hear the concern in Angelina's voice as she suggests we meet for dinner in her suite tonight. I want to say no, to curl back up in my bed and shut out the world, but something in her tone tells me she won't take no for an answer. Reluctantly, I agree.

When I show up at Angelina's suite that evening, I see the shock in her eyes as she takes in my appearance. I know I look terrible—I haven't been taking care of myself, and it shows. As we talk, she gently suggests I seek counseling to help with my grief. The idea makes me uncomfortable, but when she offers to go with me, I feel a tiny spark of hope.

The next day, we walk across campus to the counseling center. I'm nervous, but having Angelina by my side helps. For the next month, I attend counseling multiple times a week, but it feels pointless. The counselors don't understand; they can't possibly relate to what I'm going through. When one suggests I write a goodbye letter to Javier, I feel like screaming. *How can I say goodbye when I don't even know for sure if he's gone?*

During a weekend visit home, I see the worry in my mother's eyes. Before I know it, she's scheduled an appointment with a licensed psychologist covered by our insurance. To my surprise, I actually like this new therapist. The commute is long—two hours each way—but for the first time, I feel like someone might help me.

My therapist understands that without closure, saying goodbye is impossible. Instead, we work on honoring Javier's life. After several brainstorming sessions, we come up with an idea that feels right—I'll add a Spanish degree to my Special Education studies.

As I make this decision, I feel a weight lift from my shoulders. It's not closure, not really, but it's a way to keep Javier's memory alive, to carry him with me into my future. For the first time in months, I feel a glimmer of hope. It's small, but it's there, and I'm determined to hold onto it.

April 21, 1994
HONORING HIS MEMORY

With my college advisor's encouragement, I step into Sra. Santa-Madera's office in the Languages and Cultures Department, feeling a glimmer of hope for the first time in months. As she maps out a plan for adding a Spanish major, a surge of confidence fills me. This decision feels right, like I'm finally moving in a positive direction.

When Sra. Santa-Madera mentions the upcoming trip to Bayamón, Puerto Rico, my heart skips a beat. I remember my time in Ecuador and how much I learned from living among the people there. The thought of a similar experience in Puerto Rico fills me with excitement. This could be my chance to honor Javier's memory while growing as a person and future educator.

The opportunity to live in orphanages and teach English to children sounds incredible. I can feel my passion for teaching igniting within me. It's as if all the pieces are falling into place.

But the best news is yet to come. When I find out Angelina will also be part of this program, I feel a wave of relief wash over me. Having a familiar face, someone who understands what I've been through, by my side during this adventure means more than I can express.

For the first time in what feels like forever, I'm looking forward to something. The prospect of this trip, of using my skills and immersing myself in a new culture, fills me with a sense of purpose. It's not just about learning Spanish anymore—it's about healing, growing, and finding a way to carry Javier's memory with me into this new chapter of my life.

As I leave Sra. Santa-Madera's office, I feel lighter, more hopeful. The weight of grief pressing down on me hasn't disappeared, but it feels more manageable now. I have a goal, a direction, and a chance to make a difference. For the first time since losing Javier, I feel like I might be able to move forward without leaving him behind.

May 7, 1994
A NEW ADVENTURE

Stepping off the bus alongside Angelina and Ebony, I feel a surge of anticipation. We've finally arrived at Hogar Escuela de Sor Josefina, and I can hardly contain my excitement about meeting the forty-five girls we'll be working with. Even though I had hoped to work with younger children, I'm eager to connect with these teens and pre-teens.

The night air is thick with humidity as we're led through the building. I try to memorize the layout—kitchen, bathrooms, chapel—but my mind is buzzing with thoughts of tomorrow. As I'm shown to my room on the third floor, I hear muffled giggles and whispers from behind curtained stalls across the hall. My curiosity is piqued, but exhaustion soon takes over.

I wake with a start the next morning, surprised to see it's already eight-thirty. How did I sleep so soundly in a new place? As I dress quickly, I wonder how I missed the commotion of the girls getting ready for their day. The silence now is almost eerie.

Stepping into the hallway, I'm struck by the emptiness. Fifteen stalls, their white curtains neatly tied back, line the corridor. I can't resist taking a closer look. My heart pounds as I peek into each cubicle, feeling like I'm intruding yet unable to quell my curiosity.

Each tiny room gives me a glimpse into a life—posters and stuffed animals hinting at the personalities of the girls who live here. But it's the similarities that truly catch my attention—identical beds, shelves, and sparse belongings. It's a stark reminder of why we're here, of the lives these girls lead.

Taking in these intimate spaces, I'm swept away by a whirlwind of emotions: sadness at the simplicity of their lives, hope that we can truly make a difference, and a renewed determination to connect with these girls and learn their stories. This isn't just a summer program anymore—it feels like the start of something profound, something that may transform me as much as I hope to help transform their lives.

After freshening up, I make my way downstairs in search of my roommates. My heart leaps at the sight of Angelina approaching from across the room. We share excited smiles and decide to take a quick stroll outside, enticed by the warm tropical breeze flowing through the front door.

We've only walked a few blocks when the sharp crack of gunfire pierces the air. My body tenses instantly, and I turn to Angelina, my eyes wide with fear.

"Did you hear that?" I whisper, my voice trembling.

"I did," Angelina replies, her face pale.

We stand frozen, staring at each other in disbelief. It's too early for fireworks, which can only mean one thing—gunshots. My heart pounds in my chest as sirens wail in the distance, growing louder by the second. Without a word, Angelina and I turn in unison and start hurrying back to the orphanage.

As we rush past, I catch a glimpse of where the emergency vehicles are headed—a large housing complex where a crowd is gathering. My breath catches in my throat as I see a woman cradling a bloodied child, her anguished cries cutting through the chaos. I feel sick to my stomach, tears pricking at my eyes as we quicken our pace.

Relief washes over me as we reach the gates of the orphanage, but it's short-lived. A group of nuns comes running toward us, their black habits billowing as they pull us through the barricade. Two of them grab us by the elbows, their grip firm and unyielding as they march us down a long hallway like prisoners.

My mind races as we're led to the director's office. *What have we done wrong? Are we in trouble for leaving?* The stern face of the director does nothing to calm my nerves as we stand before her, breathless and uncertain.

"¡A dios mío!" she exclaims, and I watch in fascination as she makes the sign of the cross. I've seen it before but never understood its significance. As she touches her forehead, chest, and shoulders in sequence, I feel a strange mix of curiosity and unease.

Later, when I learn that this gesture is believed to drive away evil, a chill runs down my spine. The gunshots, the injured child, and now this solemn ritual—it's all so far from the world I know. I'm suddenly acutely aware of how unprepared I am for the realities of life here and how much I have yet to learn about this new culture I've immersed myself in.

As I stand there, confused and uncertain, I watch Angelina lower her head and softly utter words I don't understand: "Perdóname madre, porque he pecado (Forgive me, mother, for I have sinned)." My heart races as I realize I have no idea what's happening or how to respond. I feel completely out of my depth, like a fish out of water in this unfamiliar religious setting.

The tension in the room is palpable, and I can feel the weight of disapproving eyes upon me. A wave of shame and embarrassment washes over me as I realize they must think I'm being disrespectful or rebellious. My cheeks burn hot, and I wish I could disappear into the floor.

In contrast, Angelina seems to know exactly what to do. Her posture, her words, her entire demeanor exudes a sense of reverence and familiarity with the situation. I can't help but feel a twinge of envy mixed with admiration for her composure.

As the silence stretches on, my anxiety grows. I want to explain that I mean no disrespect, that I simply don't know the proper protocol, but the words stick in my throat. I feel like an outsider, acutely aware of my lack of religious upbringing and how it sets me apart in this moment.

The unfairness of the situation stings. *How can they judge me for not knowing something I was never taught?* Yet I also feel a deep sense of regret for not having taken the time to learn more about Catholic practices before coming here.

LESSONS FROM THE HEART

A s I stand in front of my class each day, a sense of purpose fills me. I love the freedom to create lessons and activities, watching the girls' eyes light up as they grasp new concepts. This experience confirms what I've always suspected—I'm meant to be a teacher.

In the afternoons, I find myself surrounded by eager learners seeking extra help. But I quickly realize it's more than just academic assistance they're after. These girls crave love and attention, and to my surprise, I find myself craving it too. The walls I've built around my heart since losing Javier start to crumble.

I welcome their hugs and kisses, my arms open to cradle these innocent souls. As I stroke their hair and wipe away their tears, I feel a deep connection forming. Their trust in me is both heartwarming and terrifying. I listen to their stories, my heart breaking for the situations they've escaped. I assure them of better days ahead, all the while praying I'm not giving false hope.

But not everything is rosy. Sor Hermengilde, the nun overseeing my floor, is a constant source of tension. Her strict demeanor and quick criticism grate on my nerves. Each time she scolds me for a mispronounced prayer, I feel a mix of embarrassment and anger bubbling up inside me.

I came here to teach English, not to become Catholic. At first, I tried to be respectful of their beliefs, but with each humiliation, my patience wears thin. Resentment takes root in my heart, and I find myself avoiding prayer times and ducking around corners to escape Sor Hermengilde's watchful eye.

As the days pass, I grapple with conflicting emotions. The love I feel for these girls is real and powerful, but the constant religious pressure is suffocating. I question everything—my beliefs, my purpose here, even the existence of God. *If He's real, why is there so much suffering around us?*

I'm torn between the joy of teaching and the discomfort of feeling like an outsider in this religious environment. Every smile from a student, every breakthrough in learning, fills me with purpose. But every criticism, every forced prayer, chips away at my resolve.

As I lay in bed each night, I wonder if I'm strong enough to endure this for the entire program. I'm changing, growing, but I'm not sure if it's for the better or worse. The only thing I know for certain is that this experience is shaping me in ways I never expected, and I'm not the same person who arrived here just a few short weeks ago.

May 15, 1994
SIGHTSEEING

As I step into El Yunque rainforest, my heart swells with awe. The lush greenery surrounds me, and I hear the distinctive call of the coquí frog, a sound that's become synonymous with Puerto Rico for me. I close my eyes and breathe in deeply, savoring the rich, earthy scent of this tropical paradise. When I open them again, I'm overwhelmed by the breathtaking views stretching out before me.

Later, as I swim beneath a cascading waterfall, the cool water rushing over my skin, I feel truly alive. It's moments like these that make me grateful for this experience, despite the challenges I've faced.

The Cavernas del Río Camuy leave me speechless. As I explore the underground limestone caves, I'm filled with wonder at nature's artistry. I snap picture after picture, knowing they'll never truly capture the magic of being here in person.

Our trip to San Juan is a mixed bag of emotions. Ebony's excitement at visiting the Hard Rock Café is contagious, even if the food itself is nothing special. But as we explore the busy, dirty streets of the metropolitan area, I feel a twinge of disappointment. This isn't the Puerto Rico I'd imagined.

Old San Juan, however, steals my heart. As I wander along the cobbled streets, admiring the brightly-colored colonial buildings, I'm transported to another time. The history and culture here are remarkable, and I find myself falling in love with this charming corner of the island.

May 20, 1994
LIVES CHANGED FOREVER

B each days and dance nights with the girls from the orphanage are the moments that truly touch my soul. Watching these young women, who have endured so much, finally let go of their worries and just be kids fills me with a joy that's hard to put into words. I find myself laughing and dancing alongside them, feeling a connection I never expected—a bond that transcends our different backgrounds.

Dánica, the oldest girl in the dormitory at just twenty-two, captures these precious moments with a bulky video recorder on a tripod. As I watch her, I learn that she changed her name from Monica to Dánica in memory of her twin brother, Daniel, who tragically lost his life in a drive-by shooting when they were only eight. My heart aches for her as she recounts that fateful day, and I can't help but think back to the morning Angelina and I wandered through the neighborhood, only to be startled by gunfire in the distance. It's no wonder the resident nuns and the director were so upset by our decision to explore on our own.

Dánica describes how she and her brother were walking hand-in-hand to school, blissfully unaware of the danger around them. In an instant, their innocence was shattered; a bullet struck Daniel, killing him instantly. The horror of that moment—the blood staining Dánica's crisp white shirt and plaid uniform—is a memory she can never escape. I feel a chill run down my spine, the weight of her words heavy on my heart.

But her story doesn't end there. Dánica's mother, clinically diagnosed with severe depression, never recovered from the loss of her son. Though she loved both her children fiercely, every time she looked at Dánica, she was reminded of the child she lost. The pain became too much, and after several attempts at suicide, she made the heartbreaking decision to give up her only daughter.

Hogar Escuela de Sor Josefina became Dánica's refuge. At just nine years old, she was the youngest child ever placed there. Growing up in an environment that emphasized strong Christian values, it's no surprise that Dánica chose to dedicate her life to God.

As I listen to Dánica's story, my heart breaks for her. The image of her brother's death, so reminiscent of the fear I felt, sends shivers through me. I am in awe of her strength and her ability to transform such profound tragedy into a calling to serve others.

Selena, one of my favorite little girls, has her own heartbreaking tale. She grew up in a household plagued by drugs and violence, and a fatal heroin overdose left her and her siblings orphaned. While her younger siblings were placed with family members, Selena—the oldest and only girl of eight children—was taken into custody by child protective services.

Then there are Maya and Marvelin, two beautiful daughters of a single mother who made a series of poor choices in men. After fleeing an abusive marriage, their mother entered another toxic relationship and resorted to prostitution to provide for her daughters. Unfortunately, HIV would eventually rob her of the independence she desperately sought, leaving her incapacitated and battling terminal AIDS.

While the girls still visit their mother on weekends, it's clear that time is running out. Hogar Escuela has offered them a safe haven for the past two years, fostering sensitivity during these challenging times and instilling values that will help them grow into responsible adults.

As we all sing along to "Hero" by Mariah Carey, I'm overcome with emotion. Looking around at these brave, resilient girls, I realize that they're all heroes in their own way. And in some small way, I hope I've been able to be a hero for them too, even if just for this short time.

This experience has changed me in ways I never expected. The beauty of Puerto Rico and the strength of these girls—it's all become a part of me now. As I prepare to leave, I know I'll carry these memories and lessons with me forever.

January 25, 1995
FROM FOLLOWER TO LEADER

As I immerse myself deeper into the Languages and Cultures department, I find myself forming close bonds with all my professors. Our conversations extend beyond the classroom, and, like in Ecuador, I'm often invited into their homes. It's a warmth and connection I never expected to find in academia here, filling me with a sense of belonging I've been craving since losing Javier.

My involvement in the Spanish Club becomes a cornerstone of my college experience. When I'm elected president, I feel a surge of pride and responsibility. It's as if all the pieces of my life are finally falling into place. Being inducted into Phi Sigma Iota, the honor society for foreign language students, is another validation of my hard work and passion.

As president of the Spanish Club, I throw myself into organizing multicultural gatherings, promoting holiday traditions, and sponsoring cultural performances. Each event feels like a celebration of the culture I've grown to love. When we organize trips to New York City to see plays honoring Spanish artists, I'm filled with excitement, eager to share these experiences with my fellow students.

But it's the after-school program I initiate for the children of migrant farmers that truly touches my heart.

Working with these young kids, who have no permanent home and struggle to make connections, reminds me of the girls in Puerto Rico. Their faces, full of hope and uncertainty, haunt me in the best way.

Tutoring these children in English floods me with memories from my time in Puerto Rico. But it's more than just language lessons—it's about providing a safe, welcoming space for these outsiders. Every time I greet a child with a warm smile or offer a gentle hug, I feel a deep sense of purpose. I know firsthand how powerful a simple act of kindness can be, especially for those who feel lost and alone.

As I watch these children slowly open up, see their eyes light up with understanding or joy, I'm overwhelmed with emotion. It's in these moments that I truly understand the impact of my experiences in Puerto Rico. I'm not just teaching English—I'm offering love, acceptance, and a glimmer of stability in their ever-changing lives.

This work, more than anything else, makes me feel connected to Javier. It's as if I'm honoring his memory and the lessons I learned in Puerto Rico with every child I help. And in doing so, I'm healing too, finding purpose and joy amid my own never-ending grief and uncertainty.

June 4, 1995
EMBRACING MY
BILINGUAL IDENTITY

A summer semester in Salamanca, Spain, is my final hurdle in finishing my Spanish degree and officially becoming bilingual. Living with a host family, as I did in Ecuador, I expect a similar experience, but it couldn't be more different. My roommate and I are simply tenants, given a room and three meals a day, but there's little warmth or connection from the family. It's a stark contrast to my previous homestay, leaving me feeling somewhat sad.

Despite the vibrant atmosphere of Salamanca, I find myself longing for deeper connections. Still, I refuse to let these disappointments overshadow my time in Spain. I seize the chance to travel around the country, immersing myself in its rich culture and history.

Basking in the sun on the beaches of Costa del Sol, I feel a sense of freedom and peace. The grandeur of the Great Mosque of Córdoba leaves me in awe, while the palace gardens of the Alhambra in Granada captivate my imagination. As I stroll through the medieval cities of Ávila, Segovia, and Toledo, I marvel at the Spanish synagogues and cathedrals, feeling a profound connection to the past.

In Madrid, El Prado and Paseo del Arte offer some of the best museums in the world. "The Girl at the Window" by Salvador Dalí becomes my favorite piece, its haunting beauty resonating deeply with me. In Sevilla, I fall in love with flamenco dancing; its passionate rhythms stir something within me. However, I find myself sobbing at the bullfights, disturbed by the violence and unable to reconcile it with the beauty of the culture.

Despite the differences from my previous study abroad experiences, my travels across Spain have enriched my soul in ways I never imagined. Each moment of wonder and introspection has brought me closer to my goal of becoming truly bilingual.

As I prepare to leave not just Salamanca, but also the chapter of my life that is college, I carry with me a tapestry of memories woven from both the highs and lows of this transformative journey. These experiences have shaped me, leaving an indelible mark on my heart and mind, and I know they will guide me as I step into the future.

May 5, 2015
MIND OVER MATTER

As I watch the buses depart from Edson Elementary Center and the other staff members head back inside, I linger behind, waiting for Annie Conway to catch up. The veteran teacher approaches me with a curious look.

"I didn't know you spoke Spanish," Annie says, her eyes sparkling with interest.

I smile, feeling a surge of pride. "Sí, puedo hablar un poquito de español," I respond, enjoying how the words roll off my tongue.

Annie brushes her silvery-gray bangs off her freckled forehead, looking slightly confused. "Pueblo de what?" she asks, and I can't help but giggle.

"I was just confirming your observation and saying I speak a little Spanish," I explain, amused by her attempt to understand.

"Well, thank goodness! That second grader would have been lost without you," she tells me, her tone warm with appreciation.

I nod, recalling the incident. "Today Heber had a substitute bus driver, and they sent an alternate bus. He didn't recognize the number on the outside or the driver, so he got scared. He only knows a few words in English."

"Aw, and he didn't know how to ask for help," Annie says, her voice full of sympathy.

"Exactly," I confirm, feeling empathy for little Heber. "I studied abroad in college, so I could relate to the panic I saw on his chubby little face."

As I say this, memories of my own time abroad flood back—the initial confusion, the struggle to communicate, the overwhelming feeling of being lost. I'm grateful that my experiences have allowed me to help students like Heber, bridging the gap between languages and cultures. Moments like these remind me why I became an educator in the first place.

Annie playfully bumps my shoulder, and I can't help but smile at her gesture. "Yet another of your many hidden talents," she teases, making me feel a little proud. Then she pulls out a crumpled piece of paper from her pocket. "On a different note, I wanted to share this with you."

"What's this?" I ask, unfolding the ad. My eyes scan the words "Weight Loss through Hypnosis," stirring a mix of curiosity and skepticism in me.

Annie's voice is filled with excitement. "Tomorrow night, I'm planning to attend this seminar. Care to join me?"

I pause, considering the offer. *Hmmm… Hypnosis, to help people lose weight.* My hands instinctively rest on my rotund midsection. I'm acutely aware of my short frame, flabby arms, big butt, and dimpled thighs that resemble cottage cheese. A wave of shame washes over me as I recall my doctor's words: "Being morbidly obese is harmful."

Annie's light-hearted response catches me off guard. "Think I'd go to a different doctor," she snickers, playfully touching her double chin. I chuckle, grateful for her attempt to lighten the mood.

"Well, she's not wrong," I defend, fidgeting with one of the gaping buttons on my short-sleeved blazer. The struggle with my weight weighs heavily on my mind.

Annie points to her muffin top, her voice empathetic. "For me, it's more about being able to wear comfortable clothes without going up another size."

I sigh, feeling a mix of frustration and defeat. "I've tried countless detox cleanses, pre-packaged foods, meal-replacement shakes. Nothing has worked for me."

Annie's optimism is unwavering as she focuses back on the ad. "Look, it says there's a money-back guarantee."

"It's not about the cost," I admit, my voice tinged with hesitation.

"Then what is it?" she probes gently.

I feel a knot in my stomach as I think about my husband's potential reaction. "My husband... Just one more gimmick to fall for, I'm sure he'll say."

Annie's response is quick and encouraging. "What does he know? And how do you know it won't work this time?"

I still hesitate, my mind racing with excuses. "You know how I feel about socializing with staff outside of school."

Annie's clever retort makes me smile despite my reservations. "Well, in less than a month, I'll be retired.

Then you won't be my boss anymore—you can be my 'friend'."

I can't help but grin as I watch Annie make air quotes around "friend." Her enthusiasm is infectious.

"Since you put it 'that' way," I mimic, feeling a spark of excitement despite my doubts.

"Then it's settled?" Annie's hopeful tone tugs at my heart.

"Sure," I respond, my reluctance fading under her persistence. "Since you're obviously not taking no for an answer, I guess I'm in."

As I agree, I feel a mix of nervousness and anticipation. Maybe this could be the change I need. Even if it doesn't work, at least I'll be facing it with a friend by my side.

Driving home from work, my mind races as I think about how to tell Dylan. Climbing into bed, I muster the courage to say, "I'm meeting a friend for dinner tomorrow night."

Dylan barely looks up from his phone, fingers tapping away at a text. "No problem. I'm probably getting home late anyway," he replies absentmindedly.

Just as I'm about to settle in, something on the TV catches my eye. "Look," I gasp, bringing my hand to my face and pointing at the screen with the other. The words 'Breaking News… Earthquake in Ecuador' flash across the screen.

Dylan glances up but doesn't show any real concern. "Oh, come on," he dismisses. "The place already looked like a dump anyway."

His words hit me like a punch to the gut. "I guess you forget I studied there in college," I say, my voice trembling.

A lump forms in my throat as tears trickle down my cheeks. The news anchor reports that officials are still assessing damages and determining casualties. Memories flood back of my time there—my host family and friends I lost contact with. I silently pray that none of them were affected.

Dylan, seemingly unfazed, places his phone on the charging station, turns away, and fluffs his pillow. Within minutes, he's asleep, snoring softly beside me.

I lie there, feeling a mix of sadness and frustration. The distance between us feels more profound than ever, and I wonder if he even understands how much Ecuador meant to me. As I wipe away my tears, I resolve to reach out to anyone I can remember from my time there, hoping for reassurance that they're safe.

May 6, 2017
UNLOCKING THE SUBCONSCIOUS

A s we drive to the weight loss seminar, I feel a mix of anticipation and nervousness bubbling up inside me. "There might be limited parking," I say to Annie, relieved when she accepts my offer to ride together.

On the way, we discuss our past weight loss attempts. Annie's questions spark a flood of memories, each one a reminder of my failures.

"Have you tried counting calories?" she asks.

"Yep," I reply, recalling the tedious process of logging every bite.

"Group meetings?"

"Been there," I say, remembering the uncomfortable chairs and forced camaraderie.

"Journaling?"

"Done that," I sigh, thinking of the abandoned notebooks filled with good intentions.

"Joined a gym?"

"I actually hate exercising," I admit, feeling a twinge of guilt.

Annie bursts into laughter. "Me too. My ex used to renew my gym membership every year until he realized it was just throwing money away."

Her candor makes me feel less alone. I decide to share one of my more embarrassing attempts. "Wait, I have one. No chance you've ever done this."

"Try me," Annie challenges, her eyes twinkling.

"Ever wear an iridescent spandex bodysuit and lie on a table while a technician thrusts a probe across your cellulite to freeze fat cells?" I cringe at the memory.

"Ouch! That sounds painful," Annie exclaims.

"It didn't really hurt," I explain, "but it left marks on my skin. The huge red welts faded, but the fat cells? Still there. The disappointment stings."

As we share our experiences, including Annie's cousin's bariatric surgery, I feel a growing camaraderie.

When Annie asks what I think tonight will be like, I voice my skepticism. "Dunno. We're in a group, and there's probably gonna be a lot of people. How personalized can it really be?"

Annie suggests they might ask for volunteers to go on stage. The idea fills me with dread. "God, I hope not," I say, twisting my mouth.

"You wouldn't do it?" Annie presses.

As we stop at a red light, I turn to her, my voice firm. "No way. And don't get any ideas—nobody's making a monkey out of me."

Annie's playful teasing about me strutting across the stage in my underwear makes me both laugh and cringe. "Now, that would be quite a sight," I say sarcastically as I turn into the hotel parking lot.

Despite my sarcasm, a mix of emotions churns as we park. There's hope that maybe, just maybe, this time will be different. But there's also fear of another disappointment. As we walk toward the hotel, I take a deep breath, steeling myself for whatever the evening might bring.

Upon entering the crowded ballroom after registering, my heart races. I'm already feeling exposed.

"There are empty seats up front," Annie says, pointing eagerly.

My stomach drops. I'd rather blend into the background, preferably in the last row. But I don't want to disappoint Annie, so I swallow my discomfort and mumble, "Well, here goes nothin'."

We make our way to the front, and I can feel eyes on me as we squeeze past other attendees. Just as I'm about to sit down, I hear a voice behind me that makes my blood run cold.

"I thought that was you, Mrs. Duquesne."

My cheeks flush as I realize a group of parents from school are right behind us. I want to sink into the floor. *This is exactly why I didn't want to come—* the thought of anyone from school seeing me here, admitting I need help with my weight, is mortifying.

I lean in close to Annie and whisper urgently, "If they start asking for volunteers, I'm outta here."

My heart pounds so hard I can barely hear the speaker. I try to focus on breathing, telling myself it's not as bad as it feels. But part of me is already planning my escape route. This evening feels longer and more uncomfortable than I anticipated.

As I close my eyes, I focus on my breath and the guest speaker's voice. His deep, rich tone guides us through a series of directions. "Breathe in for five; breathe out for five," he instructs. I feel the oxygen fill my diaphragm as I inhale, and as I exhale, I imagine pushing out negativity.

I can't help but peek through my eyelids. Everyone else seems to be following along. *Maybe there's something to this after all. What do I have to lose—except, hopefully, some weight?*

With each breath, I become more aware of my body. My heart rate quickens as I inhale and slows as I exhale. The deeper I breathe, the more present I feel.

Shifting uncomfortably in the hard chair, I try to find a better position. I spread my legs apart, plant my feet on the floor, and let my arms dangle. Refocusing on the speaker's words, I let go of my discomfort.

"Now, let's think of a time when you liked the way you looked," the speaker says.

I blink, startled. *Think of a time when I like the way I look?* My mind races through different periods of my life, but I come up empty. A wave of sadness washes over me.

As the presenter continues, his voice offers unexpected comfort. "Now, visualize yourself standing behind a door. As you slowly open it, find clarity through your senses. What do you see, hear, feel, taste, and smell?"

Suddenly, I'm transported. There's intense heat and dampness in the air. I hear a soft Spanish ballad, pan flutes playing in the background. Someone's fingers lace with mine, pulling me closer until I feel their cheek against mine. The scent of sandalwood—Obsession for Men by Calvin Klein—fills my nostrils. Warm breath caresses my skin as soft lips graze mine. My heart aches with longing. *Oh Javier, how I've missed you.*

"You are going to count backward from twenty to one," the speaker's voice intrudes on my reverie. "When we get to one, you will open your eyes and return to the group."

No, please don't make me open my eyes. I don't want to leave you, I think desperately, clinging to the memory of Javier.

As we reach "one," I reluctantly open my eyes, tears streaming down my cheeks. Embarrassed, I quickly wipe them away, hoping no one noticed.

"I'll be back," I whisper to Annie, my voice thick with emotion as I excuse myself to the ladies' room. My heart pounds, overwhelmed by the unexpected rush of memories and feelings. I need a moment to compose myself.

I steady myself in front of the sink, shoulders slumped and eyes wide, staring into space. My mind reels from the flood of emotions.

Annie approaches, placing a gentle hand on my forearm. "Olivia, are you okay?"

My lip quivers as I struggle to find words. "I, I don't know," I stammer, my voice barely a whisper. I catch my reflection, mascara streaking down my cheeks, and quickly wipe it away, feeling exposed. I sigh deeply and turn to face Annie. "What did you see during the session?" I ask, desperate to shift the focus.

Annie beams as she describes camping in the mountains with her boys. Her joy feels like a stark contrast to my turmoil. "And you? Where did it take you?" she asks, eyes bright with curiosity.

"Ecuador," I whisper, the word catching in my throat.

Annie smiles knowingly. "Ah, yes, one of your studies abroad. But what happened to make you cry?"

My heart clenches as I speak. "I met a man there and fell in love. It was one of the happiest times in my life." The words feel inadequate to express my loss.

"It's amazing how someone from our past can still affect us, isn't it?" Annie says, her smile warm and understanding. "You should find him online."

My stomach drops. "I wish I could," I murmur, looking down, unable to meet her gaze.

Annie gently grasps my wrist, her touch comforting. "I know you're married, but there's nothing wrong with just looking."

"I can't," I say, my voice thick with emotion.

"Why not?" she presses, confusion evident.

I take a deep breath, steeling myself. "He's dead," I blurt out, the words heavy in the air.

As soon as I say it, a mix of relief and renewed grief washes over me. It's the first time I've said it out loud in years, and the finality hits hard. I brace myself for Annie's reaction, wondering if I revealed too much.

As I watch her signal a left turn out of the parking lot, a familiar melody plays on the radio. I recognize the beautiful love song and turn up the volume, letting the music wash over me. The lyrics stir long-buried emotions.

I haven't thought about Javier in years, but now, after the hypnosis session, memories flood back—every moment, every touch, every laugh feels vivid again. I find myself lost in reminiscence, reliving our love story as I drive home.

The weight of these memories is overwhelming. Part of me wants to pull over and cry, but I know I need to get home. I'm grateful for the late hour and empty roads as I struggle to focus.

By the time I pull into my driveway, I'm emotionally exhausted. Quietly entering the house, I'm relieved to find Dylan sound asleep. I'm not ready to face him or explain my turmoil. Instead, I slip into bed, my mind swirling with thoughts of Javier and the bittersweet ache of first love lost.

May 7, 2017
AWAKENING THE SPIRIT WITHIN

I face the alarm clock, its glowing numbers mocking me—3:00 AM. Sighing, I give up on sleep and make my way downstairs to the kitchen. Cradling a hot cup of tea in both hands, I let the warm steam envelop my face and try to focus on my breathing. Inhale for five, exhale for five. But my mind keeps drifting back to Javier.

With trembling hands, I set my mug down next to my laptop and type "Javier Vargas" into the search bar. My heart races as images flood the screen, but none are him. I feel a mix of relief and disappointment. *Of course, there isn't a picture. He's dead. Isn't he?*

As I scroll through the results, a profile picture catches my eye—a young man who looks strikingly like Javier. My pulse quickens as I click on his Facebook page. He lives in Guayaquíl, Ecuador. *Could it be...?* I lean in closer, my mind whirling with possibilities, when suddenly my elbow knocks over my tea. "Ugh!" I cry out as hot liquid spreads across the table and keyboard.

"Hey, are you okay?" Dylan's concerned voice calls from upstairs.

"Yeah, I spilled my tea," I reply, my voice shaky.

I hear Dylan's footsteps rushing down the stairs. Panic sets in as I realize what's on my screen. I quickly close the window just as he appears with a pile of towels.

My robe and pajamas are soaked, but all I care about is saving my laptop. *That was too close.*

As Dylan helps clean up the mess, my mind races. *Who was that young man?* The resemblance to Javier was uncanny. *Could Javier have been married? Did he have a son?* And the question I'm almost afraid to ask myself — *Is there any chance he could still be alive?*

Twenty years ago, a stranger told me over the phone that Javier had died. I searched for answers but always came up empty-handed. Now, with this new lead, I feel a dangerous spark of hope igniting in my chest. Part of me wants to dive back into the search, to uncover the truth once and for all. But another part is terrified of what I might find.

As I help Dylan mop up the last of the spilled tea, I'm acutely aware of the weight of my secret. *How can I explain to my husband that I'm still haunted by a man from my past? How can I tell him that a part of me never stopped loving Javier?* The guilt and confusion threaten to overwhelm me, but I force a smile and thank Dylan for his help. As he heads back upstairs, I'm left alone with my swirling thoughts and the lingering question— What if?

I'm used to being the first one to arrive at school each day, aside from the head custodian. But as I turn into the long driveway, I notice another car already parked. It's Annie. My mind races with questions. *Why is she here so early? Is she waiting for someone?*

As soon as I step out of my car, Annie approaches me with urgency. "I need to talk to you," she says, her voice direct and to the point. A knot of worry forms in my stomach. Whatever it is, it seems serious.

"Let's talk in my office," I suggest, wanting some privacy for this conversation.

Once inside, I gently close the door and hang up my coat, while Annie settles into the chair across from my desk. Her presence feels heavy with anticipation.

"You're scaring me. What's wrong?" I ask, my voice tinged with concern.

Annie leans forward and whispers, "I'm here to deliver a message."

"A message? From who?" I ask, curiosity piqued and a hint of apprehension creeping in.

"Before I share who sent me, I want to ask if you've ever heard of reiki," Annie says.

"Ray key? How do you spell it?" I ask, unfamiliar with the term.

"R-E-I-K-I," she spells out.

"No, I've never heard of reiki," I admit, feeling a bit lost. "What is it?"

"It's a type of energy healing," she explains.

"I'm completely confused. Energy healing? What does that even mean? What does energy healing have to do with me?" I ask, bewildered by the direction this is taking.

Annie's words hit closer to home than I expected. "Last night, you shared with me that someone you loved very much unexpectedly died. You were left with many unanswered questions."

A chill runs down my spine, and my eyes widen. "This is neither the time nor place to talk about this," I protest, feeling exposed.

"Please, just hear me out," Annie pleads, her sincerity evident.

I take a deep breath, trying to steady myself as I prepare to listen to what she has to say, my emotions swirling with a mix of fear, curiosity, and a glimmer of hope.

Over the next twenty minutes, I give Annie my undivided attention. I'm intrigued by what she has to say. Although I can't fully comprehend the impact that reiki has had on her life, I acknowledge that the practice provided her with the comfort she needed after her son passed away.

I don't know enough about the healing technique to support it. However, I can't criticize or disregard such a practice either.

"My guides are telling me that it's time. Javier wants to talk to you," Annie says.

Javier wants to talk to me. How in the world is that even possible?

Before leaving her office, Annie hands me a post-it and strongly suggests I call the number neatly written in the center of the patriotic star to schedule a session with Raquel, her reiki master.

I take the note with trembling hands, feeling a whirlwind of emotions. Skepticism battles curiosity, fear battles hope. *Could this really be a way to connect with Javier after all these years? Or am I setting myself up for more heartache?*

As I watch Annie leave, I'm left holding this small piece of paper that suddenly feels like it weighs a ton. I know making this call could change everything, and I'm not sure if I'm ready for that. But the thought of possibly hearing from Javier again... it's almost too much to resist.

Throughout the morning, my mind is consumed by my conversation with Annie. The curiosity gnaws at me, and by noon, I can't resist any longer. *What do I have to lose?* I tell my secretary that I'm making an important phone call and shouldn't be interrupted.

With a deep breath, I close my office door, dim the lights, and sit back down at my desk. Carefully, I dial each digit from the small piece of paper Annie gave me.

As the phone rings, a strange sense of familiarity washes over me when I hear Raquel's voice, even though we've never spoken before. It's comforting yet unsettling.

Raquel mentions she's leaving for a two-week vacation over the weekend. She suggests we could wait until she returns, but encourages me to come for a session before she leaves. Her words linger in my mind, and I feel a pull to act now rather than wait.

Javier wants to talk to me. The thought echoes in my mind, both thrilling and terrifying. *How could this be possible?* Yet, the hope of connecting with him, even in some small way, is too enticing to ignore.

Before ending the call, Raquel's gentle encouragement convinces me to schedule a session. As I hang up, a mix of anticipation and anxiety fills me. *This could be the closure I've been seeking, or it could unravel emotions I've kept buried for years.*

I sit quietly for a moment, staring at the phone, feeling the weight of what I've just set in motion. The idea of possibly hearing from Javier again brings a flutter of hope, but also a fear of reopening old wounds. Yet, I know deep down that I need to take this step, to explore whatever answers or peace it might bring.

May 8, 2017
A HEARTFELT REUNION

I arrive at my appointment a full thirty minutes early, a habit born from my need to be punctual and my fear of getting lost. Raquel practices reiki out of her home, and I can't exactly stop to ask for directions if I take a wrong turn. Only Annie knows where I am, and that thought both comforts and unnerves me.

As I pull into the driveway, I see Raquel outside, tending to her garden. She's wearing a sleeveless beige maxi dress and sandals, her long, wavy auburn hair pulled back in a loose ponytail. Her presence is calming, and I feel a strange sense of familiarity, even though we've never met before.

"Hi, Olivia! How are you today?" she greets me warmly.

I take a deep breath, trying to steady my nerves. "Ready," I reply, though my voice betrays my anxiety.

Despite just meeting, there's an inexplicable comfort in Raquel's presence. I'm usually so guarded about my past, but with her, I feel an unexpected trust.

Raquel welcomes me into her home and leads me down a hallway. She opens the last door on the right, allowing me to enter first. I take a moment to absorb my surroundings: a candlelit room with soft instrumental music playing, sheer curtains swaying gently in the breeze, and the sweet scent of lavender filling the air.

The room is simple, with a massage table in the center and shelves lined with stones, gems, and crystals. Votive candles flicker softly, and watercolor paintings with Chinese symbols adorn the walls. I wonder about their significance but am too anxious to ask.

Eager to start, I ask, "Can I use your bathroom?"

"I was going to suggest that," Raquel replies kindly. "When you're ready, come back across the hall, take off your shoes, lie on the bed, and make yourself comfortable."

I nod and head to the bathroom, trying to calm the gnawing pain in my stomach. *Please don't make me have to go to the bathroom during the session,* I silently plead.

Returning to the room, I lie down fully clothed, my arms pressed firmly by my sides. I stare at the intricate designs on the ceiling tiles, trying to distract myself from the nervous anticipation. As I wait for Raquel to return, I can't help but wonder what this session might reveal and if it will bring me any closer to the answers I've been seeking.

Raquel gently closes the door behind her, and I feel a mix of anticipation and skepticism. "My hands will be positioned close to your body, but we won't actually touch," she explains softly.

Since this is my first session, she suggests starting with a body scan. "Rei, meaning universal, combined with ki, signifies life energy," she says. "So this is a practice where positive energies will be exchanged with intention."

As she places her hands, palms facing downward slightly above my body, she continues, "I'll be able to identify areas in need of attention." Her voice drops to a faint whisper, instructing me to close my eyes and focus on the music.

"You wear contacts," she states matter-of-factly.

My eyes snap open in surprise. *How does she know I wear contacts?* "I do," I admit cautiously.

"Has your left eye been bothering you?" she asks.

"No," I reply, puzzled.

"It soon will. There's a slight tear in the lens," she predicts.

I take note of her observation, unsure if I should believe it, but intrigued nonetheless.

"I can feel warmth coming from your abdomen. You've had surgery in this area, which has left you with extensive scar tissue," she continues.

Dumbfounded by her accuracy, I squint with my right eye, opening the left one just enough to see Raquel standing above me, eyes closed, hands hovering as she said they would be.

"The surgery was for your liver?" she inquires, her voice calm and certain.

How could she possibly know this? "Yes, I had half of my liver removed when I was in high school," I confirm, my voice barely above a whisper.

"The tumor was benign. And they removed your gallbladder at that time too?" she asks.

"Yes," I say, feeling a mix of disbelief and awe.

Raquel also mentions my unsettled digestive issues, and before I can respond, I unexpectedly burp, relieving the knot in my stomach. Embarrassed, I feel my face flush.

"I'm sensing inflammation in your knee and ankle joints, possibly from a recent fall," she continues.

"Hm… About a year ago, I stumbled and twisted my ankle. I landed on concrete and skinned my knees," I admit, my mind racing with thoughts of how she could possibly know all these things about me. It's strangely surreal, and I can't help but feel a sense of wonder at Raquel's gifts.

"Now, the real reason you were sent to me," Raquel says, her voice taking on a deeper, more serious tone. My heart skips a beat as I brace myself for what she might reveal next.

As I lie there, eyes closed, I suddenly feel a presence in the room. My heart races as tears begin streaming down my face. *It's Javier. I can feel him next to me; he's holding my hand.* The sensation is so real, so familiar, it takes my breath away.

Raquel's voice breaks through my emotional haze. "I'm here to serve as the go-between. You'll pose a question in your mind, and I'll verbalize the answer."

My mind immediately forms the question I've been carrying for years: *What happened?*

"I was killed by two men," Raquel says, and I feel my heart shatter all over again.

Why? I think desperately.

"They knew I had a large sum of money. They followed me, robbed me, and then murdered me."

The revelation hits me like a physical blow. *Why were you carrying so much money?* I ask silently, dreading the answer.

"I wanted to be with you. Applying for visas didn't seem to be working out. While I knew that it was dangerous and illegal, I saw no other way."

I gasp, struggling to catch my breath. The weight of his sacrifice, his love, and the tragedy of his fate overwhelm me.

I feel Raquel's hand on my forearm. "I know, sweetheart. It's a lot to take in. Just know I'm here for you," she says softly.

Then, I feel Javier's touch—his hand stroking my arm, his finger caressing my face. The warmth of his breath tickles my ear as he whispers, "I'm always with you and will love you forever, muñeca."

"Muñeca," I choke out. "It's what he used to call me." No one had ever made me feel so beautiful, so cherished as when Javier called me his doll.

Uncontrollable sobs wrack my body, leaving me breathless. As I struggle to refocus, I sense a change in the room. The warmth of Javier's presence fades, as if he's vanishing into thin air.

"I'm so sorry," Raquel says softly, but I know these are Javier's words as much as hers.

Even though his spirit is no longer in the room, I can feel the lingering imprint of his love. The closure I've sought for so long mingles with fresh grief, leaving me raw and vulnerable. But beneath it all, there's a glimmer of peace, knowing that Javier's love for me never wavered, even in death.

May 9, 2017
DIGITAL FOOTPRINTS

Lying next to Dylan, my mind is consumed by thoughts of Javier. Unanswered questions swirl, refusing to let me rest. *Murdered over money... Why would he risk crossing the border illegally? So many make the journey every day. Why him? I was saving money, working hard. It might have taken longer, but I was confident we would eventually be together. Am I to blame for his desperation?* I remember the heartbreak when his second visa was denied, and I can't help but wonder if my impatience pushed him to take such a dangerous path.

The image of a young man online who looks so much like Javier haunts me. I can't shake the feeling that there's more to this story, something I'm missing. *Did the spiritual connection with Javier really happen, or was it just my imagination?* But then there's the coincidence with my contact lens, just as Raquel said.

Unable to sleep, I slip out of bed, my heart pounding as I tiptoe downstairs. This time, I'm extra cautious with my cup of tea, remembering my earlier mishap. The night is quiet, but my mind is anything but. I sit in the dim light, sipping my tea, and wonder if I'll ever find the answers I seek.

With trembling fingers, I log into my Facebook account and search for the young man—Javier Vargas. My breath catches as I see his timeline: this 'Javier

Vargas' was born after my Javier had already died. A chill runs down my spine as I click on 'See Javier's About Info.'

Under 'Family Members,' my heart skips a beat at the name 'Valería Vargas,' listed as his mother. Curiosity overwhelms me as I navigate to Valería's page, where I find numerous albums of pictures. The photogenic mother of three bears a striking resemblance to my Javier. *Could she be related?* My mind races back to Javier mentioning his siblings. *Is it possible this is his younger sister?*

Gathering my courage, I decide to reach out. With shaking hands, I type a message asking if she has a brother named Javier. As I hit send, a mix of anticipation and fear washes over me. I sit on the edge of my seat, anxiously refreshing the page, hoping for a response.

Throughout the day, I log onto my account repeatedly, each time met with disappointment. Doubt creeps in. *Can she even see my message? Is she ignoring me?* The uncertainty gnaws at me.

Determined, I take a different approach. With a lump in my throat, I upload a picture of Javier and me from our last night together. Memories flood back as I attach it to a new message, asking Valería if she knows the Javier Vargas in the photo.

The wait is agonizing. Nearly twenty-four hours pass, each minute feeling like an eternity. Then, suddenly, a notification. My heart races as I open the message.

Valería's response sends a jolt through me: "Mi hermano se llamaba Javier!!!" Her brother's name was Javier. I can barely breathe as I read on.

"La foto que adjuntaste al mensaje es de mi hermano!" The photo I attached is of her brother. My hands shake as the reality sinks in.

"Tu fuiste su amiga?" She wants to know if I was his friend. *Friend? Oh, if only she knew.* Tears well up in my eyes as I struggle with how to respond, the weight of our shared connection to Javier overwhelming me.

Speaking in Spanish, I tell Valería I met her brother during the summer of 1993 while studying at the university. I explain that the photo was taken in front of Laica University and that I'm the woman standing beside him.

Valería shares that her brother died twenty years ago. She is his younger sister, and they were very close. She named her eldest son after him because he will always hold a special place in her heart, not just as her brother.

I tell Valería I have many wonderful memories of her brother, and hearing about his death was incredibly difficult for me. I recount how, twenty years ago, I was caught off guard when I called Javier's apartment, and a woman answered, telling me he had died. I ask Valería if she can tell me how he died and if she has a copy of the obituary.

Though Valería reads my additional messages, she doesn't respond. Opening this door to the past was unexpected, but since Javier's sister engaged in conversation, I remain hopeful.

May 25, 2015
THE SELF-LOVE CHALLENGE

A s soon as Raquel returns from her vacation, I eagerly head back to see her. With her guidance, I learn to communicate with Javier, something that once felt impossible but now comes surprisingly naturally. Once I open myself to the possibility, I find it easier than I ever imagined.

Over the years, I sensed Javier's presence countless times. I remember believing he was hiding in the bushes, convinced he had found a way to be with me illegally. Deep down, I knew the answers to my questions long before I was ready to accept that he was gone. Handling large sums of money often made me uneasy, perhaps a lingering connection to the circumstances of his tragic death.

Now, more attuned to his presence, I recognize the signs he sends me through songs on the radio. Specific rhythms remind me of the Latin music we once danced to, while certain lyrics evoke memories tied to our time together. The presence of Ecuadorians at the schools where I work feels significant, as if they are messengers connecting me to Javier. Occasionally, a child's name or a fleeting memory from my travels brings a rush of nostalgia.

Raquel introduces me to chakras, explaining that they are spinning wheels of energy along the spine that affect nearby organs. A blocked chakra can disrupt this flow, which is how she sensed issues with my left eye, scar tissue in my midsection, digestive problems, and joint inflammation.

During our reiki sessions, Raquel focuses on unblocking my chakras to allow energy to flow freely. Unsurprisingly, my heart chakra requires the most attention.

On the outside, I've built a successful career, taking on leadership roles by thirty. But those accomplishments came at a cost. The harder I worked, the more responsibilities I took on, leaving me feeling like a hamster on a wheel—constantly moving but making no personal progress. In the midst of all this, I lost my way.

Raquel's voice breaks through my thoughts. "I want you to look in this mirror and tell yourself that you are beautiful," she instructs. Her request seems simple, yet it feels impossible. A tear escapes as I look at her, the weight of disbelief heavy on my heart.

"Go ahead, I want to hear you say the words out loud," Raquel encourages gently.

"I can't," I whisper through tears, unable to lie to myself or her.

"Perhaps you can't now, but you will," she reassures me. "Between now and our next session, look in the mirror daily and say, 'I love you.'"

Her words linger in my mind, a challenge and a promise of healing. As I leave, I carry the hope that one day, I will embrace those words and truly believe them.

May 28, 2015
Helping Me Find Myself

I take everything Raquel suggests seriously. So, I do exactly what she tells me. Once a day, I force myself to stand alone in front of the mirror and try to say those three words.

I love you.

On the third day, as I stand in the small bathroom on the first floor, I'm suddenly not alone. "Te quiero, mi muñeca," I hear Javier say.

The floodgates open, and I start sobbing uncontrollably. I'm grateful to be alone, with no one else to see me make such a spectacle.

"Déjame escucharte decirlo," he instructs gently.

"I love you," I whisper, my voice barely audible.

"Otra vez, y más fuerte," he urges.

"I love you," I repeat, a little louder this time.

With Javier's encouragement, I gradually learn to say it with conviction. His presence, even just in spirit, gives me the strength I need to believe those words.

Regular reiki sessions with Raquel help me heal physically and emotionally. Over time, I feel more relaxed than ever. I sleep soundly through the night and experience less stress during the day. Raquel teaches me to meditate, empowering me to continue my journey toward peace.

As I practice these new habits, warmth grows inside me. It's as if Javier's love and Raquel's guidance are helping me rediscover a part of myself I thought was lost forever. Each day, as I look in the mirror and say those three words, I feel stronger and more whole. The journey is far from over, but for the first time in years, I feel hope blossoming in my heart.

August 10, 2015
THE WEIGHT OF SILENCE

After all these years, I've miraculously connected with Javier's younger sister online and finally confirmed his death. Yet, the questions of how, when, and why remain unanswered. I scour online newspapers from Ecuador, hoping for any clue that might shed light on what happened to Javier. After months of searching during every free moment, I still come up empty-handed—no articles, no obituary, nothing to provide the closure I desperately seek.

Valería, Javier's sister, has accepted my friend request. I take this as a good sign, a glimmer of hope. I message her, trying to express my gratitude without coming off as too pushy. I know she might be my only chance for answers. I start by thanking her for accepting my request and complimenting her beautiful family, hoping to open the door to a deeper conversation.

As I wait for her response, my mind races with possibilities. *What if she holds the key to understanding what really happened?* The anticipation is almost unbearable, but I know I must be patient. This connection, however fragile, feels like a lifeline to the past and the truth I've sought for so long.

When Valería responds almost immediately, my heart races. She sends her regards, and I feel a glimmer of hope. She thanks me for the picture, saying it brought back good memories. My stomach tightens, sensing her hesitation to elaborate further.

Feeling guilty for possibly upsetting her, I quickly type an apology, explaining that I have so many questions about Javier's death. My fingers tremble as I hit send, hoping she'll understand my need for closure.

Valería's reply is swift and cuts deep. She reminds me that she doesn't know me and firmly states she no longer wants to talk about or relive her brother's death. Before I can process her words, she signs off, leaving me staring at the screen in disbelief.

A wave of disappointment washes over me. Of course, I've never met Valería, and I'm unsure what, if anything, Javier ever told her about our romance. I can understand why she'd be guarded, but it doesn't make the rejection hurt any less.

Discouraged but not completely disheartened, I force myself to concede. I know I need to accept that Valería doesn't want to discuss the details of her brother's death. The fear of her unfriending or blocking me, cutting off access to those precious family photos and posts, keeps me from pushing further.

December 23, 2015
A Season of Silence

Over the next four months, I admire Valería's new posts and photos from a distance. As Christmas approaches, I can't resist reaching out with a simple "Feliz Navidad." As I type, I hold my breath, hoping this time she'll respond. But as the seconds tick by after I hit send, that flicker of hope dims, and my heart sinks.

My holiday greetings go unanswered, leaving me feeling discouraged. It's as if my words vanished into a void, swallowed by unspoken grief. I sit there, staring at the screen, feeling the ache of rejection seep into my bones—a cruel reminder that some connections are just out of reach.

December 20, 2016
CAPTURED MOMENTS,
SILENT HEARTS

E ach new picture fills me with hope that this year Valería might finally respond. I see her smiling with family, celebrating cherished moments together. With a mix of anticipation and trepidation, I type out "Feliz Navidad," my heart racing as I hit send.

But as minutes turn into hours, then into days, nothing comes. The silence is crushing, a heavy weight settling in my chest. I stare at the screen, feeling disappointment wash over me. It's as if my words have vanished into thin air, lost in the vastness of her life that I can only observe from afar. Each moment without a response deepens the ache in my heart, reminding me of the connection I long for but can't seem to grasp.

December 21, 2017
GHOSTED: THE ART OF DISCONNECTION

I keep scrolling through Valería's posts, my heart aching as I read each holiday greeting she shares. "Feliz Navidad," I type again, hoping this time will be different. But as the days pass, my message remains unanswered.

I feel like a ghost, lingering on the edges of her life, desperately trying to reach out but never truly being seen. The joy in her posts feels like a bittersweet reminder of unanswered questions, and the absence of a response only deepens the loneliness wrapping around me like a heavy blanket.

I can't help but wonder if I'll ever break through that barrier.

December 25, 2018
WHEN WORDS GO UNREAD

I still send my annual holiday message, clinging to the hope that this year will be different. Each time I type out "Feliz Navidad," a mix of anticipation and dread washes over me. But now, looking at my message, I see it hasn't even been read; the little notification that indicates she saw my words is absent, and my heart sinks further.

At least she hasn't blocked me as a friend, I remind myself, but that thought offers little comfort. The silence is deafening. I feel like I'm shouting into a void, my words disappearing without a trace. Each unacknowledged message chips away at my spirit, leaving me more heartbroken than ever.

I want to reach out, to connect, to share memories of Javier, but it feels like I'm trapped in a one-sided conversation. The weight of unreciprocated feelings hangs heavy in the air, and I can't shake the feeling that I'm losing my chance to bridge the gap between us.

The holidays come and go, but the emptiness remains—a constant ache in my heart.

December 20, 2019
LEAP OF FAITH

As I scroll through Valería's updated posts and photos, my heart skips a beat when I notice a new name on her page—Lorenzo Vargas Soto. I immediately recognize him from family photos Valería has shared before. He's one of Javier's brothers.

For the next twenty minutes, I'm consumed by indecision. *Should I send a private message to Javier's brother?* My mind races with possibilities and fears. *What if he rejects my request to talk? What if he ignores me completely? But then again, what if he responds?*

Taking a deep breath, I decide to take a leap of faith. With trembling fingers, I type out a message in the app:

"Saludos. You are a brother of Javier Vargas. Is that correct?"

As soon as I hit send, doubt floods my mind. *Should I have written it in Spanish? What if Lorenzo doesn't speak English?* I consider resending the message in Spanish but stop myself. There are translation apps if he needs them, and sending a second message so quickly might make me look desperate.

I toggle anxiously between my email and social media messages, my stomach in knots as I wonder how long it will take him to respond. *Does he check his messages every day? Is he even logged on right now?*

With each passing minute, my anticipation grows. I can't help but imagine all the possible outcomes. This could be my chance to finally get some answers about Javier, to fill in the gaps that have haunted me for so long. But it could also open old wounds, bringing back the pain I've worked so hard to overcome.

I find myself holding my breath every time I refresh the page, hoping to see a response. The waiting is excruciating, each second feeling like an eternity. This small message carries so much weight—it's a bridge to the past I've been longing to cross, yet terrified to approach.

As I wait, I'm a bundle of nerves and hope, teetering on the edge of a potential breakthrough or heartbreak.

It takes exactly forty-six minutes for him to reply. My heart leaps as I see Lorenzo's message pop up on my screen. "Yes, I am," he writes. "I know you? Or you were a friend of my brother?"

My hands trembling, I quickly type back, explaining that I was Javier's friend, that we met during the summer of 1993 when I was studying in Ecuador. Lorenzo's surprise is evident in his response, and I can feel my own excitement building.

When he asks for a clue, I take a deep breath and upload the picture of Javier and me from our last night together. As I share the details of when and where it was taken, tears start to form in my eyes.

"Never seen this picture before," Lorenzo replies. "Brought me a lot of memories. Thank you so much for sharing."

Overcome with emotion, I start to cry. "Your brother was such a beautiful person, inside and out," I type, my vision blurring.

I can't believe it. After all these years, I've finally connected with another member of Javier's family. I'm actually communicating with one of his brothers. My mind races with all the things I want to say, all the questions I've been holding onto for so long. I try to temper my eagerness, not wanting to come on too strong, but also desperate not to lose this opportunity.

For the next hour, Lorenzo and I reminisce about Javier. We talk about how we met, about Javier's work at the market, about his English classes. With each detail Lorenzo confirms, I feel a piece of my past clicking into place.

"I loved your brother very much," I confess. "I've lived my life believing he was my soulmate."

As our conversation deepens, I feel an inexplicable connection with Lorenzo. It's as if we've known each other for years, despite never having met. When I finally gather the courage to ask about Javier's death, Lorenzo's openness takes me by surprise.

He shares the exact date of Javier's death and where he's buried. As we exchange stories, I find comfort in our shared memories and different perspectives. When we sign off, promising to talk again tomorrow, I feel a sense of peace I haven't known in years.

The next morning, I wake up with an unfamiliar serenity. *Was it all a dream?* I quickly check my phone, relief washing over me as I see our conversation from the night before.

Without hesitation, I initiate another chat. When Lorenzo responds almost immediately, I feel a surge of hope. I take a deep breath and ask the question I've dreaded for so long: "What happened to your brother?"

Lorenzo's answer is both a confirmation of my worst fears and a relief to finally know the truth. As he shares details about the men who murdered Javier and the family's struggle to cope with the loss, I feel a mix of grief and gratitude.

When Lorenzo promises to try and find Javier's obituary, I'm touched by his willingness to help, even as he explains the difficulties of broaching the subject with his mother.

His confession that the family hasn't spoken of Javier in years breaks my heart, but I understand their pain. As our conversation draws to a close, I feel a bittersweet mixture of closure and renewed grief. But underneath it all, there's a sense of connection—to Javier, to his family, to a part of myself I thought I'd lost long ago. For the first time in years, I feel like I'm finally starting to heal.

December 21, 2019
SEARCHING FOR SOLACE

K nowing why Lorenzo is hesitant to discuss his brother's death with their mother, I'm utterly shocked when I read his next message.

"I talked with my mom about you," he writes.

Even though Javier's mother never met me, she knew about me. Her son had fallen in love with an American girl and dreamed of going to the United States.

"Did you show her the picture?" I ask, my heart pounding.

"I did," Lorenzo replies. "I haven't seen that smile or the brightness in her eyes for so long."

Tears stream down my face as I take a picture of the card I received from Javier on our last evening together and upload it. On the back of a business card, he had handwritten a message that professed his love for me.

As Lorenzo shares Valería's suspicions, I feel a mix of understanding and regret. "I completely get why Valería would be hesitant to trust a stranger," I say, my voice laced with empathy. "If the situation were reversed, I probably wouldn't have even accepted the friend request."

I take a deep breath, feeling vulnerable. "I don't have a profile picture, events, or photos on my Facebook page because I'm an elementary principal. Because of my job, I'm cautious about publicizing my private life."

As I say this, I realize how much I've kept hidden, not just online but in life.

Lorenzo's understanding warms my heart, and when he confides that he was initially hesitant about my message, I feel a connection growing between us. "You messaged me on the exact same day I made my page public," he reveals, and I can't help but marvel at the coincidence.

"Was it a coincidence?" I ask, my voice barely above a whisper.

His next words fill me with a sense of belonging I haven't felt in years. "For this very reason, I knew it was meant to be, and I'm so thankful I trusted my instincts," Lorenzo says. "As far as I'm concerned, you're officially a part of our family."

Tears prick at my eyes, and I need a moment to compose myself. Before we end our chat, I gather my courage and ask, "Do you think Javier's younger brother, Mateo, might talk with me?"

My heart races as I wait for his response. "You mentioned you were much older than Javier. Mateo and Javier were closer in age and very close. He might have known about our romance."

As I wait for Lorenzo's answer, hope and anxiety swirl within me. The possibility of connecting with someone who might have known about Javier's feelings for me all those years ago thrills and terrifies me. It's another step toward uncovering the truth about our past, and I find myself holding my breath, hoping for a chance to piece together more of the story that has shaped so much of my life.

December 22, 2019
UNEARTHING THE HEADLINES

When Lorenzo signs onto Facebook, my heart leaps as he tells me he and Mateo are together. Mateo knows the photo is real. Although he can't recall me, he followed the love story and has every reason to believe it's true.

I'm baffled by the timing of events. *Why is this all happening now?* The question echoes in my mind, and I can sense that everyone, including Mateo, is wondering the same thing. *What does fate have in store for us? What's going to happen next?*

My breath catches as Lorenzo's next message appears: "I got the newspapers. They'll help you understand that fateful night. Let me warn you, it looks gruesome. I don't recommend looking at it."

They've found the documents I've been desperately seeking for all these years. My stomach churns as Lorenzo warns me about the graphic nature of the pictures. I know Ecuadorian newspapers can be explicit, leaving nothing to the imagination. The descriptions of Javier's death are likely to be horrific. Despite this, a part of me knows I need to see the headlines and stories reported to the people of Ecuador.

"My heart is racing," I type, my fingers trembling. "While I don't want to see the pictures, I need to. Please forward them to me."

I explain my past efforts. "I traveled to the Library of Congress in Washington, D.C., years ago, but I had no idea what I was looking for. I've searched on and off for years, looking for answers. And now I find you. Thank you!"

Hours pass without a response. As my eyelids grow heavy, I drift off to sleep, thinking, *I have waited twenty-five years for answers. What are a few more hours?*

Dylan has no idea about any of this, and for now, I intend to keep it that way. Maybe it's better that Lorenzo hasn't sent the pictures yet. Seeing them will undoubtedly be emotional, and Dylan would immediately sense something was wrong. He'd ask questions—questions I'm not ready to answer yet.

As I lie in bed, my mind races with anticipation and fear. The truth I've sought for so long is within reach, but I'm terrified of what I might discover. *Will these answers bring closure or open old wounds?* Either way, I know my life is about to change dramatically, and I'm not sure if I'm ready for what comes next.

IN THE GRIP OF DARKNESS

A s I wake to the sound of the garage door closing, I remember Dylan mentioning he'd be going into the office for a few hours. My heart races as I reach for my phone, hoping for a message from Lorenzo.

His words pop up on the screen: "Sorry, I fell asleep early. I get your eagerness, but it was painful for me."

Taking a deep breath, I scroll down and see four pictures uploaded to my iPhone. My hands tremble as I realize I now have full access to the front-page news that exposed the horrific accounts of what was presumed to have happened that fatal night.

The first picture shows the front page of a newspaper—a photograph of investigators examining the inside of a vehicle, with the headline reading, "Tres muertos sentado en un Suzuki!"—Three dead bodies found seated in a Suzuki.

I gasp, breath catching in my throat as I recognize the vehicle. It's the same car Javier drove when we were together—the same car I rode in to and from his apartment on our last night together. The reality of it hits me like a physical blow, far too close to home now.

Sitting alone on the edge of the bed, tears well up from deep inside as thoughts race through my mind. Everything I've been searching for all these years is finally starting to surface. *Am I really ready for this? If not now, then when? Should I be tackling this alone? If not alone, then with whom?*

I think of my best friends — one in Florida, the other more than three hours away. Dylan's at the office, which is actually a blessing in disguise. I'm grateful for the solitude in this moment.

Like ripping the Band-Aid off an old wound, I scroll on with caution and trepidation. Despite Lorenzo's warnings about the painful pictures and grotesque sights, nothing could have possibly prepared me for the second picture — a photo of Javier's lifeless body lying on a black and white striped blanket.

My heart shatters all over again as I stare at the image. The finality of it all crashes over me in waves of grief and shock. I want to look away, but I can't. This is the truth I've been seeking for so long, and now that it's here, I feel overwhelmed by the weight of it. Tears stream down my face as I grapple with the reality of Javier's death, now undeniably real before my eyes.

As I stare at the horrifying image on my phone, it slips from my trembling hands and clatters to the floor. The dam inside me breaks, and tears stream uncontrollably down my face. I bend to retrieve my phone, but a wave of dizziness hits me, and I sink to the floor, gasping for breath.

Wiping my tears with the sleeves of my pajama top, I force myself to continue, though every fiber of my being wants to look away. The colored ink emphasizes the gunshot wound to Javier's head, blood running down his face and neck. Puddles of blood soak into what looks like a bedspread, and red debris – *oh God, is that brain matter?* – lies scattered on the fabric.

Through my blurred vision, I notice something hauntingly familiar. My heart races as I bring the picture into focus. *Could it really be?* The bedspread in the photo looks just like the black and white comforter from Javier's bed—the bed we shared on our last night together.

Frantic, I scroll back through my conversations with Lorenzo. It was the same bedding! The realization hits me like a physical blow: Javier was robbed and murdered in his own apartment, then taken to where he was found with two other bodies. Those monsters must have used his own comforter to wrap him up.

I crawl back into bed, pulling the covers over me as I continue to sob. *Why? Why did they have to kill him? If it was just about the money, couldn't they have just robbed him? Did Javier fight back? Did he struggle?*

The image of the gunshot to his head burns in my mind. *Was he shot anywhere else? Was it quick, or did he suffer?* Each question spawns another, and I feel like I'm drowning in a sea of unanswered horrors.

I remember that night during the reiki session when Javier's soul connected with mine. He told me he had found a way to come to the U.S. illegally after his visa applications were denied. He mentioned men had followed him, knowing he had a large sum of money. Were these the same men who promised to bring him here?

Suddenly, nausea overwhelms me as a familiar, gut-wrenching question resurfaces: *Was I the reason Javier was dead?* The weight of guilt and grief threatens to crush me as I lie there, alone with my thoughts and the brutal reality of what happened to the man I loved.

The pain is far too much to bear. I cradle my phone in my arms, close to my heart, and cry myself to sleep.

Four hours later, I'm startled awake by my cell phone vibrating on my chest. I blink, disoriented, and look at the screen. It's 12:17 PM.

How long was I sleeping?

It's Dylan calling, probably from the office. I answer with a sheepish "Hello."

"Olivia, is that you? Did I wake you?"

I feel a flicker of annoyance. *Who else would it be? Dylan and I are the only two people living in our home. Our cats can't answer the phone, so of course, it's me.*

"Yes, it's me," I say, sitting up in bed. I explain that I must have fallen back to sleep.

"It's afternoon. Are you okay?" His concern is evident in his voice.

"Yes, I'm okay," I lie. "I have an upset stomach. Maybe I caught something from work."

"The guys and I were going to work a few more hours and then grab a bite. Do you want me to come home?"

"No, you go. Have fun. I'll be fine." Given my emotional state, more time alone would actually be a blessing. I still have no idea how to tell Dylan what happened.

"Are you sure?"

"Yes, I'm sure. Tell Dave and Tom I said Merry Christmas."

"Okay, I'll call you on my way home."

After hanging up, I get out of bed and head to the bathroom. Despite the small white lie, I really do have an upset stomach. After brushing my teeth and washing my face, I grab my cell phone and go downstairs.

I put a piece of bread in the toaster and place a teapot with water on the stove to boil. My head is pounding, so I take two aspirin, hoping they'll help. I'm hopeful that the toast and a hot cup of green tea will settle my stomach.

As I wait for the water to boil, I lean against the counter, my mind racing with thoughts of Javier, the horrific images I've seen, and the weight of the truth I now carry *How am I going to process all of this? And how am I possibly going to explain it to Dylan?* The emotional turmoil threatened to overwhelm me again, but I take a deep breath, trying to focus on the simple task of making tea. *One step at a time, I tell myself. One moment at a time.*

Referring back to my phone, I revisit the two pictures that haunt me. A caption in smaller print reads, "Los tres cadáveres, aún deter del Suzuki, en la Y de la vía a la costa donde aparecieron." My heart races as I translate it in my head—*readers could read on to find out more about the three cadavers found in the Suzuki on the road next to the coast.*

The third upload is an actual news report. The headline reads, "Misterio en crimen de Suzuki: Cuatro asesinados en 48 horas." A chill runs down my spine as I translate: "Mystery in the Suzuki crime: Four murdered in forty-eight hours."

As I read through the police report, my stomach churns. Organized crime has struck Guayaquil, with four people killed within 48 hours. They were apparently murdered in various sectors of the city, but all victims were allegedly prosperous merchants from La Bahía.

My eyes sting with tears as I read about Javier Antonio Vargas Soto, a second-year student of Foreign Trade at Vicente Rocafuerte Laica University and a prosperous merchant of La Bahía. His mother's words pierce my heart—she couldn't understand why he was killed. "He was a calm and hardworking young man. My son was not a criminal, nor did he have enemies," she had said.

"Javier's poor mother," I whisper, my voice breaking. I can't imagine what it must have been like for her to find out her son was murdered. Seeing these pictures and reading these articles today is dreadfully heartbreaking for me; I can only hope reliving this awful discovery hasn't been too difficult for her.

As I continue reading, my hands shake. He was kidnapped. Even the investigators weren't clear about what happened, but police reports indicated theft. Yet, Javier still had his documentation, jewelry, and watch. Nothing makes sense.

Then I see it—a beautiful picture of Javier, so vibrant and handsome. The caption beneath identifies him as Javier Antonio Vargas Soto, a young merchant who was kidnapped, killed, and found in the interior of his own car. My heart aches at the sight of him, so full of life in this photo, knowing the brutal end that awaited him.

The final picture is almost too much to bear—a graphic black and white image of multiple men in uniform lifting a dead body, wrapped in a blood-stained sheet, from the Suzuki. I force myself to read the details of the victims' injuries, my stomach turning with each word. When I read about the victim with a bullet hole in his jugular, another in the head, and one in his right shoulder, with his right hand totally destroyed, I know it's Javier. A sob escapes me.

Lorenzo's words after the pictures hit me like a physical blow: "The sadness covers our hearts. By this dust of guessing his final minutes. Rest in Peace, Javier Vargas."

I curl up on the couch, hugging myself tightly as tears stream down my face. The reality of what happened to Javier, the man I loved, is almost too much to bear. The brutality, the senselessness of it all—it's overwhelming. I feel a deep, aching sorrow not just for Javier, but for his family, for all the years lost, for the future that was stolen from him. And beneath it all, a gnawing guilt that I can't shake. *Could I have somehow prevented this if I had done something differently?* The weight of these emotions threatens to crush me as I lie there, alone with the brutal truth I've sought for so long.

As I type my messages to Lorenzo, my heart is heavy with a mix of gratitude and sorrow. I feel unusually comfortable asking him questions, but I'm acutely aware of the need to respect his family's privacy. I don't want to come across as disrespectful or find personal peace at the expense of their grief. A nagging worry tugs at me—*I hope sharing these articles hasn't been too unsettling for them.*

With trembling fingers, I type: "I'm sorry for any sadness I brought to your family by having you relive the awful murder. I thank you for trusting me and providing the answers I've searched for all these years."

Tears well up in my eyes as I continue: "As I shared with you before, I loved your brother very much. He was such a beautiful person, both inside and out. I was a young, shy girl studying in a foreign country. I always felt safe with your brother."

My heart swells with bittersweet memories as I describe our connection: "I was learning Spanish; he only knew a few words in English, but we were still able to communicate. His larger-than-life personality drew me in and gave me no choice but to trust him. I have trusted him all along, which led me to you and this moment."

A sense of profound gratitude washes over me as I type: "I have no doubt he brought us together. Your brother has, and always will be, the greatest gift of my life. Thank you to you and your family for sharing him with me."

When Lorenzo replies with "Thank YOU. You brought me pride to be the brother of an excellent human being," I feel a warmth spread through my chest. His words about not knowing Javier well due to their age difference and living in different countries make me realize how much this connection means to him too.

As Lorenzo describes Mateo's close relationship with Javier, I find myself relating deeply to Mateo's personality. The image of the yin-yang symbol flashes in my mind, representing the balance between Javier and those who loved him. It's a bittersweet realization of how we were all interconnected through Javier.

Lorenzo's next messages hit me like a physical blow: "He felt his heart scattered after my brother passed away. It took years to recover."

My heart aches for Mateo, imagining the depth of his pain and devastation. The revelation that the family worried about his suicidal thoughts sends a chill down my spine. I'm overwhelmed by the ripple effect of Javier's loss, feeling both grateful for the connection I've found and deeply saddened by the enduring pain his family has experienced.

I remember the first time I saw Mateo's name on Facebook. His profile picture was an image of Al Pacino as Tony Montana from *Scarface*, holding a gun. It was intimidating and disturbing, which is why I hesitated to send him a message.

The silhouette I chose for my profile was quite different, meant to protect my anonymity. Mateo's choice projected a persona I found unsettling, and I realize I have fallen into the trap of judging a book by its cover.

When Lorenzo tells me he showed our chat to Mateo, he mentions that Mateo was surprised by how long our conversation was.

"You mean the amount of time? Number of messages? Or both?" I ask, curious about what caught Mateo's attention.

"Amount of lines," Lorenzo replies. "Because I was translating and got tired."

I wonder aloud if Mateo might talk with me. Lorenzo explains, "He is not a talker like me. His English skills are not good. I would like to involve my siblings."

I feel a pang of disappointment but understand. "I have patiently waited 25 years for this," I say, hoping to convey my willingness to be patient.

Lorenzo reassures me: "But they don't feel confident about their English skills. I guess it's a big barrier. Even I felt that way. You made me gain confidence."

"Your English skills are great!" I reply, wanting to encourage him.

"You flatter me," he says, and I can sense his smile through the screen.

Naturally, I provide reassurance and encouragement. Having studied a second language myself, I know how difficult it can be, and I admire anyone willing to try.

"I cherish our friendship," Lorenzo says.

"Me too," I reply warmly. "I enjoy hearing about your family."

Talking with Lorenzo has become a cherished part of my day, sometimes multiple times a day. He shares pictures of his children and videos of his adorable twin grandsons. Though he often says I flatter him, the truth is, I feel privileged to call him my friend.

December 24, 2019
BREAKING BARRIERS

M y heart races as I type the message to Lorenzo: "Mateo accepted my friend request!"

Lorenzo's response is immediate and enthusiastic: "Oh, that's great news!"

I feel a mix of excitement and nervousness as I clarify: "Mateo and I never actually talked, though. He just accepted my friend request."

Lorenzo's reply makes me smile: "You'll be a real challenge for him. I want him to write and chat with you. But he's so scared."

I hesitate, not wanting to push too hard: "I'll probably reach out again. I don't want to annoy him. But if he reaches out to me, I'll gladly talk."

As Lorenzo describes Mateo as naive and shy, I feel a wave of empathy. I remember how shy I was when I first met Javier.

"When you talk with him, let him know that I'm nobody to be afraid of," I type, hoping to ease Mateo's apprehension.

I share my experience with Valería, feeling a sense of accomplishment:

"Valería once avoided me too. It makes me happy that she responds to my messages now. I don't talk with her as much as I do with you."

Lorenzo's response warms my heart: "I'm not closed-minded. I'm not a restrictive person. But you make me feel so confident. And through you, I understand a lot about my little brother. I've changed my attitude around them."

With a deep breath, I start to recount my last interactions with Javier: "I spoke with him for the last time in December of 1993. My birthday is in January. He said he sent something to me. Nothing ever came."

As I type about my attempts to reach Javier, the old pain resurfaces: "When I returned to college, I tried calling him. But I never got an answer. I left messages, but he never returned my calls."

My hands tremble as I describe learning of his death: "In April, a woman answered the phone. I don't know who she was. She told me he died. A close friend who spoke native Spanish came and talked to her to confirm what I heard. I was in shock and completely devastated."

Lorenzo's suggestion about his father in New York surprises me: "Maybe he asked our father, who used to live in New York, to buy your gift?"

I feel a mix of curiosity and sadness as I learn this new information: "I didn't know your father lived in the United States. Where?"

As Lorenzo explains his father's movements from Florida to New York, I can't help but wonder how different things might have been if I had known this years ago. The emotions are overwhelming—hope, regret, curiosity, and a deep longing for answers that have eluded me for so long.

As I read Lorenzo's messages, my heart aches with a mix of sadness and newfound understanding. I had always assumed Javier was drawn to New York City for its tourist attractions and skyscrapers, but learning that his father had lived there throughout most of Javier's teenage years adds a whole new layer of meaning to his dreams.

"It must have been so challenging for your parents," I type, my fingers trembling slightly, "with your dad living and traveling between two countries all the time."

Lorenzo's response hits me hard: "He was forced. They had two or three bank accounts. Here, those banks declared bankruptcy. They froze all the money many merchants had."

My mind reels as I try to process this information. "So they lost their money?" I ask, feeling a wave of empathy for the hardships Javier's family must have faced.

Lorenzo's words paint a stark picture: "Merchants without money are nothing. It's shameful to admit, but it happened. So at least half a million people left the country. Twelve years later, they paid."

As I learn about the financial crisis in Ecuador during the early eighties, my heart breaks for Javier's family and all the others who faced such devastating losses. I can almost feel the desperation that must have driven Javier's father to leave his homeland and seek stability in the United States.

The image of Javier's father living in a small studio apartment, saving most of what he earned to send home to his wife and six children, brings tears to my eyes. I realize now that Javier's dream of coming to the U.S. wasn't just about adventure or romance—it was deeply rooted in his family's struggle and resilience.

When Lorenzo mentions Javier's visa application being denied, I feel a pang of regret and sorrow. "We met in May," I type, my heart heavy. "He died in January."

Lorenzo's next message fills me with bittersweet warmth: "I'm pretty sure that if my brother had gone to the U.S., you would have been the first person he met."

As I picture Javier going to the consulate in Guayaquil, applying for a visa on his own without seeking guidance from his family, I'm struck by his independence and determination. I wish I could go back in time, to be there for him during that process, to offer support or just hold his hand.

The weight of all this new information settles on my chest. I feel a deep connection to Javier's family history now, understanding the context of his dreams and aspirations in a way I never did before. It's bittersweet—this knowledge brings me closer to him in some ways, but also underscores the tragedy of his loss and all the potential that was cut short.

As I process this new information about the visa application, I feel a mix of frustration and sadness. I can't help but imagine Javier navigating this complicated system, trying to make his dreams a reality.

"It confuses me why he didn't list his father as his sponsor," I type to Lorenzo, my mind racing with possibilities. "He was already living here."

Lorenzo's response is a stark reminder of the complexities of immigration: "Because he wasn't a citizen. My father only had a visa."

"That makes sense," I reply, feeling a pang of disappointment.

As Lorenzo explains further, "So no tourist or merchant can request it. Only a citizen can," I feel a wave of realization wash over me.

This conversation brings home the harsh realities of immigration laws and their impact on families and relationships. I think about Javier, trying to navigate this system alone, perhaps too proud or scared to ask for help. I wonder how different things might have been if he had reached out to his father or if I had known more about the process back then.

The weight of all these "what ifs" settles heavily on my heart. I'm grateful for Lorenzo's openness in sharing these details, but each new piece of information also brings a fresh wave of grief for the future Javier and I never got to have. It's a bittersweet feeling—understanding more about Javier's world and the challenges he faced, while also being painfully aware of how much was lost.

March 1, 2020
TIME TRAVELERS

Four months after my first conversation with Lorenzo, Javier's younger brother Mateo finally accepted my friend request. My heart raced with anticipation, but I knew that language barriers and conflicting work schedules would be a challenge. It took another two months before we could actually connect. Unlike my frequent chats with Lorenzo, Mateo and I had to schedule our conversations in advance.

When the day finally arrives, I nervously type, "Buenos días."

"Hola!!" Mateo replies, and I feel a flutter of excitement.

His next message touches me deeply: "Me satisface mucho saber que los recuerdos de mi hermano no se hayan olvidado a pesar de tanto tiempo." He's pleased that the memories of his brother haven't been forgotten despite the passage of time.

But then his tone shifts, and my heart aches as I read: "Para mí, recordar a mi hermano es un poco triste porque vivimos muchas cosas juntos y porque quedó impune ante la ley ése crimen." For him, remembering his brother is bittersweet, as they experienced so much together, and the crime remains unpunished.

I take a deep breath, trying to formulate my response in Spanish. "Hablo mucho con Lorenzo," I write, explaining that I often talk with Lorenzo. "Me encanta escuchar historias sobre él." I love hearing stories about Javier.

As Mateo begins sharing memories, I feel a mix of joy and sorrow. He tells me about being fifteen, with Javier at sixteen, assigned to the same classroom after their family moved. I can almost picture them, young and full of life, navigating classes together.

When Mateo describes their family's struggles and move to Quito, my heart breaks for them. I imagine Javier, vibrant and curious, struggling to find his way in the rigid school system. The image of the brothers being taunted for looking different brings tears to my eyes.

But it was Mateo's recollection of the fight that truly rattles me. As he describes Javier gasping for breath, unable to throw punches, I experience a profound sense of fear and sorrow. The high elevation had played a role, and I recall the disorienting sensation when we drove through the mountains.

"He could do nothing," Mateo writes, and I can hear the pain.

Overwhelmed by emotion, I sit back, letting the weight of these memories settle over me. Through Mateo's eyes, I see a new side of Javier—not just the man I loved, but the brother, the student, the fighter. I can clearly visualize what I assume to be a boxing match.

My heart races as I imagine Javier struggling for breath in Quito's high altitude. I don't condone fighting, but I know it's not unheard of among boys. How ironic that Lorenzo often described Javier as a rascal who rarely turned down a dare.

I can't help but smile at Lorenzo's description of Javier and Mateo as partners in crime, like Batman and Robin. But my smile fades as I consider the tragic irony—Javier's life was lost in a way eerily similar to Batman's weakness: allies turning against him. The men he trusted to bring him to the United States were the same ones responsible for his demise. My stomach churns at the thought of their betrayal.

When I mention Javier trying to come to the U.S., I reflect on the ignorance of youth, not realizing the dangers they would face. I'm moved by Mateo's insight and the wisdom he's gained through this painful experience.

He tells me that Javier had a strong desire to migrate to the U.S. to grow economically and follow their father's example. I'm overwhelmed by a mix of pride in Javier's ambition, sorrow for dreams cut short, and a deep regret that I couldn't have done more to help him achieve those dreams safely.

This conversation with Mateo is both healing and heartbreaking. Each new piece of information helps me understand Javier better, but also reminds me of the future we'll never have. I'm grateful for Mateo's openness, even as I struggle with the weight of these revelations.

As I reflect on Javier's character, my heart swells with admiration and concern. He was strong-willed, ambitious, and impulsive—always leading with his heart. I can't help but smile, thinking about how he'd jump in without thoroughly thinking things through. It was just like him.

With his father living in a different country, Javier took on the role of the man of the house. But it breaks my heart to think of him shouldering such responsibilities at a young and sensitive age. He was far too young to take on that burden.

Looking back now, I feel a pang of regret. To think he was ready to make life-changing decisions... it fostered a level of self-confidence that was both boastful and dangerously naive. I wish I had known, so I could have been a voice of reason to protect him from the weight of those choices.

Tears well up in my eyes as I type: "Realmente creo que es Javier quien nos trajo a todos juntos." (I really believe it's Javier who brought us all together.)

Later, as I share my conversation with Mateo with Lorenzo, I'm overwhelmed by the emotions flowing through our exchanges. Lorenzo's words about their hearts healing and feeling proud to remember Javier fill me with bittersweet warmth.

Lorenzo expresses how different it feels now to talk about Javier and how it makes him feel proud. I'm struck by the power of shared memories and shared grief. Through all this pain and loss, Javier has indeed brought us together, creating connections that span decades and continents. In this moment, despite the lingering sadness, I feel a profound sense of gratitude for the love that continues to bind us all.

April 15, 2020
NEW CHAPTER

Day after day, I find myself eagerly communicating with Lorenzo. Every morning, I wake up and quickly check my phone to see if he has messaged me. Throughout the day, I keep an eye out for new messages, and even at night, I chat with him while lying next to Dylan in bed.

"I really enjoy talking to him and his siblings," I confide to my friend Annie, "and I feel disappointed when he's not around."

Annie looks at me with a hint of concern. "Has it affected your relationship with Dylan?" she asks gently.

I pause, thinking back to the other night. "I must have been dreaming, talking in my sleep," I whisper. "I woke up to Dylan wrapping his arms around me, kissing my forehead, and telling me he loved me."

Annie nods. "Do you think you were telling him in your dream that you loved him?"

"Yeah, I'm sure I probably did," I admit, a hint of guilt creeping into my voice.

"And Dylan thought you were saying it to him?" she asks, raising an eyebrow.

I bite my fingernails, a nervous habit I can't quite shake. "Possibly. Is that bad?"

Annie pauses, considering her response. "Well, I guess it depends. Have you lost interest in Dylan or fallen out of love with him?"

I straighten up, feeling a rush of emotion. "That's the thing. I actually feel like we've grown closer since this whole reunion started."

"Really? How so?" Annie asks, genuinely intrigued.

I take a deep breath, my mind flashing back to the struggles Dylan and I faced. "As you know, we struggled with fertility issues for years. After countless failed pregnancies, it really took a toll on our marriage—physically and psychologically."

It was true. Making love had turned into a mechanical process focused solely on conceiving. Each failed attempt chipped away at my desire to even try. When Dylan reached out to me, I would push him away, the emotional rollercoaster too much to bear.

But now, with the connection to Javier's family, something has shifted. Revisiting the past has allowed me to heal parts of myself I didn't realize were broken. It's brought Dylan and me closer, reminding me of the love we share and the strength we have together.

As I reflect on those difficult years, my heart aches with the memory of the pain and isolation I felt. I pulled away from everyone—my husband, friends, colleagues, and family. They had no idea how excruciating it was for me to attend baby showers, birthday parties, and other celebrations of new life. Working in a school, surrounded by hundreds of children, staff, and parents needing my attention, was a daily struggle. And Mother's Day? God, that was the worst.

There just weren't enough hours in the day to meet all the demands of my principal position. The more I produced, the more was expected of me. The more time

I spent at work, the less time I had for myself. I felt like a hamster running on a wheel, exhausted but going nowhere. Over time, I lost my way.

I was always tired and run down. Whether it was the lack of physical activity or mental motivation, it was a vicious cycle. Many days, I was downright miserable. At work, I perfected the ability to make others believe I was a strong, self-confident woman. But behind closed doors, I was an unhappy grouch. Dylan took the brunt of it. He tried to be encouraging, but he just didn't understand.

After twenty-five years, I finally had answers. With closure came the ability to grieve, releasing a huge weight I didn't even realize I'd been carrying for so long. Reminiscing about cherished memories from a time when I actually loved myself helped me immensely.

Lorenzo, a romantic at heart, shared names of different musicians and music he listened to. I found myself drawn to many of these selections, especially those with instruments from Ecuador. On any given day, I'd softly play background instrumental music with pan flutes by Leo Rojas in my office.

As I enjoyed the music, I noticed others were intrigued by the unique sounds. Their interest sparked questions and led to conversations. Most people had no idea I studied abroad in college or that I was bilingual. Their impressed reactions made me feel good about myself—something I hadn't experienced in a long time.

This journey of reconnecting with my past through Lorenzo and his family has been bittersweet but also healing. It's as if rediscovering these parts of myself has awakened something in me, reminding me of the person I used to be—someone who loved life, who had dreams and passions. Maybe I can find my way back to that person again.

As I began connecting with people, I discovered we shared many uncommon commonalities—struggles with body image, fertility, losing weight, and making time for self-care, to name just a few. It was comforting to know I wasn't alone in these challenges.

One day, a teacher at school asked if I had ever tried Zumba. Knowing my reluctance about any aerobic exercise in a group, she quickly mentioned that the instructor offered virtual classes. "I never even turn on my camera," she said, handing me a link. "Just try it."

Not only did I try it, but I also loved it. The cardio routines incorporated Latin-inspired dance—salsa, merengue, and bachata, among others. Although I never met the instructor, she was extremely encouraging, calling out my name in a fun-loving way during the hour-long workout. I enjoyed these classes so much that they became part of my weekly ritual—Tuesdays, Sundays, and occasionally a 'pop-up' on Saturdays. It became a priority in my life, and nothing interfered with Zumba.

"You say Javier was the love of your life. How do you think Dylan would feel if he knew that?" a friend asked me one day.

"Javier changed my life and gave me direction," I explained. "He lifted me up when I was questioning who I was and what I wanted to do. He gave me a confidence I never knew I had. He was my first true love. I truly believe Javier is my guardian angel and orchestrated this reunion. He knew I was close to hitting rock bottom and needed to be lifted up."

"And what about Dylan?" she pressed.

"My love for Dylan is beyond measure," I replied, my voice filled with emotion. "He inspires me. He gives me space when I need it but never lets me fall. He pushes me to be and do better. He is more than just a husband—he's my closest confidant and best friend."

"You're publishing a book, a very personal story about another man you romanticize—someone Dylan doesn't even know about. How do you think he'll feel?" she asked, concern in her eyes.

"I honestly don't know," I admitted. "He knew I was writing a book and wholeheartedly supported me throughout. I offered several times for him to read it, and I worked most of the time at our kitchen table on the initial manuscript. He had full access to it anytime."

"Do you think he read it when you weren't around?" she asked.

"Sometimes I think so, but other times I'm not sure," I confessed.

"If roles were reversed, would you be upset?" she inquired.

"You know, I've been asked that often. I really don't think so," I said thoughtfully. "My relationship with Javier happened long before I met Dylan. Why would there be a need to be jealous? Everyone has past relationships."

"But you wrote a book about another man," she pointed out.

"Yes, but I think it's important to understand how and why it came to be," I explained. "Initially, it started as sharing cherished memories. Friends and colleagues, along with his older brother, suggested I consider making it a book. It was emotionally challenging, and I thought about giving up many times, but I did it for his family—as a tribute to show them how much of an impact Javier made on my life. After sharing it with close confidants, I was encouraged to pursue publishing."

"I really think your story can inspire and empower others," she said, her voice filled with encouragement.

"That is exactly what I hope to achieve," I replied, feeling a sense of purpose and determination.

Epilogue
A LOVE THAT TRANSCENDS TIME AND DISTANCE

Grief is the last act of love we may have to give to those we loved.
Where there is deep grief, there was great love.
                                        - Unknown

To say that one person is more affected by the death of another could be presumptuous and offensive to some. Likewise, the idea that everyone grieves in the same way is irrational. I know this all too well now.

Miraculously, after twenty-five years of searching for answers, Javier's family and I were finally able to piece together the puzzle. Separated by two hemispheres, it was Javier's unwavering love and devotion that brought us together, enabling us to support one another as we grieved.

The summer of 1993 may be seen by some as merely a snapshot in time. For me, it marked the beginning of a journey that would change my life forever. Left physically scarred at such a young age, I became preoccupied with the fear of always being seen as disfigured and undesirable.

Javier single-handedly captured my attention, providing unconditional love and hope that a long-distance relationship could defy the odds. When tragedy struck, the absence of hard facts made it impossible for me to say goodbye.

Steadfast and resilient, I honored the love of my life by pursuing a degree in Spanish, building a career in education, and nurturing a passion for forging uncommon connections with others. My eclectic interests and open-mindedness eventually guided me to an unconventional reunion.

Though technology can often feel impersonal, social media connected me to Javier's siblings—first Valería, eight years later Lorenzo, and shortly thereafter Mateo. Individually, we camouflaged our grief in different ways, never fully mourning the loss of our loved one. Social networking provided us the opportunity to bond over shared memories, allowing us to finally grieve and discover peace from within, together.

Javier's untimely death left Mateo feeling angry, helpless, and confused. His older brother was his hero and protector. Without Javier's presence to shield him from tormentors, he struggled to find a way forward.

The fact that the perpetrators of such a heinous crime got away with murder is unfathomable. No sentence can replace the life stolen from us on that fateful day, and to believe that Javier isn't haunting them in their dreams is naïve.

Years ago, I befriended Annie, a retired reading specialist who buried not one, but two children. Her story taught me that grief knows no bounds, and everyone's pain is unique and valid.

Out of the blue, my correspondence with Javier's mother—who had long ago lost her son to the past—was surreal. More than once, she had to pinch herself to ensure it wasn't an illusion. Unexpectedly, it brought her comfort to receive a previously unseen photo of her son, smiling beside his love—a picture of the handwritten card he had given to his sweetheart professing his love. Most enlightening for her was learning that, even after all these years, I still referred to him as the love of my life. No greater gift could be given to a bereaved mother.

As I watch Valería regularly share precious photos on her timeline—friends and family celebrating milestones and special occasions—I admire the closeness of Javier's family from afar. Slideshows set to music reveal that Javier's mother, the matriarch, is consistently surrounded by love from her children and grandchildren.

Through this journey of reconnection and healing, I've come to understand that grief is a complex, ever-evolving process. It differs for everyone, yet it has the power to unite people in unexpected ways. Through our shared love for Javier, we've found a way to keep his memory alive and support each other in our ongoing journey of healing.

Valería was always comfortable showcasing her life online, but when it came to her beloved brother Javier, she was extremely guarded. Despite his vibrant personality, it felt as though the joy and laughter he brought into their lives were buried with him the day he died.

Over time, I began to look forward to logging onto social media during and after special occasions, specifically to see the pictures and videos Valería posted. It was my way of keeping a piece of Javier close to my heart.

Nothing touched me more deeply than the Mother's Day video posted on May 10, 2020. It featured two pictures of Javier among fifty-eight other cherished memories in a two-minute cinematic masterpiece titled "Live the Moment." I quickly reached out to Valería, expressing how much I enjoyed the video and how moved I was to see Javier included.

I had no idea my spirits would be lifted even higher. Valería responded, revealing she had found more pictures of her brother. She attached five precious mementos: a photo of Javier with his brothers, a headshot of him in a suit and tie, a snapshot of him standing above bright city lights, a print of him showing off a large bottle of liquor, and a pose in naval uniform beside their mother.

I did a double take when I saw the picture of Javier in uniform with his mother. Just two months earlier, his nephew—named after him—posed in a similar picture with their grandmother. The expression on Javier's mother's face in that photograph was likely one of pure exhaustion, as he made silly faces beside her. I imagined she wished he could settle down for just one moment to take the ceremonious event seriously.

Seeing these images and sharing these moments with Valería brought bittersweet comfort. It was as if, through these memories, Javier was still with us, continuing to unite us even after all these years.

As Lorenzo reflected on my relationship with Javier, he felt a deep sadness. It pained him to admit he didn't really know his brother. In his eyes, Javier was merely a mischievous rascal lacking maturity and self-control.

He remembered how often he got into trouble and how punishment seemed ineffective.

Despite the grief he caused our mother, Javier was still thought to be her favorite. Lorenzo now says I am the light that illuminated his brother's virtues. Listening to my stories, he realizes with a heavy heart that he clearly misunderstood Javier's intentions.

Lorenzo listens as his siblings recount tales of Javier's kindness and sensitivity towards their mother, who ruled with an iron fist. He's moved to hear that after work, Javier would often be waiting for her, taking off her shoes, helping her find a seat, and bringing her a container of hot water to relieve her swollen feet. These stories paint a picture of the brother he never knew, leaving him with a mix of regret and admiration.

He's struck by how Javier and their mother instinctively understood one another. They didn't hold grudges and easily offered forgiveness for each other's shortcomings. He views this journey of discovery as bittersweet, confiding, "While I'm grateful to learn about this side of Javier I never knew, I can't help but feel a deep sense of loss for the relationship we could have had. Yet, through these stories and memories, I feel like I'm getting to know my brother all over again, and in a way, it's bringing us closer even now."

No one will ever know what really happened in those final moments of Javier's life. As I think of him, my heart swells with memories of his larger-than-life personality and that infectious laugh that could light up a room. Javier had an American dream, burning with ambition and carrying himself with a confidence I admired.

To me, Javier was the love of my life. I can still feel the electricity of that summer day in 1993 when fate brought us together. I was just a shy, innocent exchange student in a foreign country, but from the moment our eyes met, it was love at first sight. The magic between us was like something out of a fairytale—a connection so pure and intense that it took my breath away.

As I sit here, my heart aching with the weight of what could have been, I find solace in the knowledge that our connection continues to stand the test of time. Even now, after all these years, I feel Javier's presence in my life, guiding and inspiring me.

It's difficult to say what might have been if things had turned out differently. But one thing I know with absolute certainty is that the love Javier and I shared was real, powerful, and everlasting.

Rest in peace, Javier Antonio Vargas Soto. You may be gone from this world, but you will forever live on in my heart and in the hearts of all those whose lives you touched. Your spirit, your laughter, your love— they continue to echo through time, a testament to the beautiful soul you were and the lasting impact you've had on all of us who were lucky enough to know you.

Acknowledgments

I would like to extend my heartfelt gratitude to my family for their unwavering support of my dream to study abroad. Reflecting on that journey, I can only imagine the nerves you must have felt.

A special thank you to my host family for graciously welcoming me into your home. Your kindness and warmth have left a lasting impression on my heart.

To my friends and colleagues, thank you for listening intently to my story and encouraging me to put it into words. Your patience and steadfast support throughout the various drafts and revisions have been invaluable.

I am also deeply appreciative of beta readers and fellow authors. Your insightful feedback and guidance have been instrumental in shaping the narrative.

This story, though tinged with tragedy, would not exist without the charismatic Guayaquileño who captured my heart over twenty-five years ago. The tales shared with his family played a crucial role in mending a broken spirit.

Lastly, I want to express my profound gratitude to my husband. Even if you never read this book, your unconditional support means more to me that words can convey. Thank you for being my rock.